FORESHORE
Classic Short Fiction

About
Toby Wilsher

Toby Wilsher lives in West Sussex on the south coast of England, where his debut novel *Snake Town* is set. After working as a cleaner in a psychiatric hospital, and manning the tills at a record shop, he embarked on a Performing Arts Degree at Middlesex Polytechnic before founding the Trestle Theatre Company in 1981. Over the next twenty-three years, he was an actor, writer, maker, designer and director for Trestle, seeing his work performed in 31 countries. Since 2004 he has worked as a freelance director, writer and corporate trainer.

TOBY WILSHER

SNAKE TOWN

FORESHORE PUBLISHING
London

Published by Foreshore Publishing 2022.
The home of quality short fiction.

Copyright © Toby Wilsher 2022

Foreshore Publishing
The Forge 397-411 Westferry Road,
Isle of Dogs, London, E14 3AE

Foreshore Publishing Limited Reg. No. 13358650

ISBN 978-1-9168790-5-8

www.foreshorepublishing.com

Acknowledgements

"SNAKE TOWN, aka BOGNOR DOGS has had a long gestation. I co-founded Trestle Theatre Company in 1981, and our stage Manager Paul Gee recommended we look at John Maddison Morton's one-act play 'BOX AND COX', itself a rewrite of 'FRISETTE', an 1843 French vaudeville piece. The basic structure revolved around a landlady and her daughter renting out an apartment to two men who never meet, hence the phrase, to 'box and cox'. We never took up Paul's offer, but years later, in 2009 I was commissioned to write and direct a play for the State Theatre of Turkey in Erzurum. I took the basic premise of 'BOX AND COX' and wrote 'SEYTAN AYRINTIDA GIZLIDIR', or 'DEVIL IN THE DETAIL'. Returning to the UK I remounted and toured the play and visited the Edinburgh Festival as Metamorpho Theatre Company. And that was that. But the story has stuck with me, and after several iterations as a novella, I combined the story with some other ideas mooted previously with my friend Steve Crossley. We'd spent some hours chewing over narratives based in Bognor Regis, again, too good to throw away. So, a big thank you to all these people, Paul Gee, Steve Crossley, Sezai Yilmaz and everybody at Erzurum DT, and the UK cast and crew of James Greaves, Alan Riley, Michelle Baxter, Sarah Thom, David Clarke and Jack Read. But mostly to my wife Kathryn who has held the fort – and the children – while I gadded about the place pursuing the elusive Rosie and Ludmilla." TOBY WILSHER, JUNE 2022.

PART ONE

*"Fear is the white lipp'd sire
Of subterfuge and treachery."*
Lydia Sigourney.

"Bugger Bognor"
George V.

NOVEMBER 2, MORNING.

ROSIE

As Rosie stared into the mirror on the morning of her 21st birthday, she was momentarily consumed by a sense of doom. It was not unusual, this fleeting pulse of adrenalin and cortisol. It had been a grumbling constant for over a year and had started with her mother's current money-making scheme.

The thought of her mother expelled the panic, to be replaced by a niggle of irritation. How might her life have turned out had her stubbornly Ukrainian mother, Ludmilla Shatalova, realised how inappropriate her name was when she decided to settle in Bognor Regis? Maybe Rosie would have had more friends, maybe she wouldn't have grown up an angry, potty-mouthed harridan that sent every man packing. She might even have become the catwalk model she yearned to be, but she held her name responsible for Elite London not plucking her from salty obscurity (ignoring the fact that she was more plus-size than heroin chic). As a young girl growing up in the southern beach resort of West Sussex, she was often confused by teachers mangling her surname, putting the stress on the first syllable to make acceptable the unacceptable. She became Chatoliver, or Chatalover. Then one day she found her surname had mysteriously disappeared, never to be spoken again in school, and she became Rosie Miller in a confused nod to her mother, Ludmilla. But it was too late. Her name followed her like a bad smell, and though she soon forgot her scatological matronymic and its smirk-inducing pronunciation, children will be children and such juicy information was never going to disappear. It was finally at a sleep-over in her last year at Nyewood Junior school that her three so-called besties revealed how her name had been received in those early cruel years.

"Shatalova! Shat all over? Are you kidding me?" screeched the appalled 10-year-old Rosie just as they were tucking into 300g of pink shrimps and a bag of mix-up allsorts on Shania's bed.

"Well, how does your mum say it?" asked Tia, spearing a sugary imitation decapod with a stiletto nail decorated luminescent green and attendant faux diamonds.

"I dunno. Can't understand a word she says, it's all slurred this and 'my dahlink' that. Don't recall her ever actually saying her surname."

"Is it, like, her name or your dad's?" asked Keeley, who always wanted to know the provenance of everyone's dad, as her mother was hazy on the details of her XY chromosomal donor. As in, 'why can't you remember his name...?'

"I literally have no flippin' idea" said Rosie, dramatically. The gaps in her pre-pubescent teeth were filling up with pink gunk, giving her a garish clown-like look when she bared her teeth. Shania looked thoughtful.

"But then you became Miller, but we all knew. Maybe you should ask your mum to change yer name, you know, like, by.... what's it called?"

"Deed-poll" said Tia, an expert on having to change your name quickly to avoid county court judgements.

"Nah", dismissed Rosie, "that would mean my mum having to do something, like, y'know, official. I swear to god she's here illegally."

Her Birthday, the 2nd of November. She had worked out some years before that her conception was because of either a bawdy Christmas bash or an out-of-control new year's shindig. Either way, she was an accident. Her mum was very hazy on anything to do with her life back in the Ukraine.

It was early morning, a Tuesday. The weak late autumn sun never reached her bedroom. The only room with natural light in their basement flat very much belonged to Ludmilla,. The luminescent glow of the digital clock was her only window into the temporal world. 6.59am. She reached over and turned the alarm off before its insistent bleep jarred her eardrums, and she simultaneously switched the radio on. Radio 1 Extra. A grime artist she didn't know banged on about a stabbing in the Old Kent Road with a verbal dexterity to rival Shakespeare, but with the musical wherewithal that made Plastic Bertrand sound like Vivaldi.

She peeled back the leopard-print duvet and slipped into a pair of fiendishly expensive Louis Labaria slippers, shrugged on her D&G dressing gown over her sheer Victoria's Secret Camisole and stood in front of the mirror. 21 today. Tall, broad shouldered and curvy, her hair had been much-dyed over the years so it's natural lustrous black sheen was now a straw-like blonde. The harsh ceiling lights cast shadows around her morning-soft skin and cornflower blue eyes.

"Christ, I look at least 30" she thought, trying to smooth away the bulging belly – pregnant? Fat chance of any bed action for Rosie this last year. No, this belly was born of beer and grease, indulgent pastries, and frozen Cook curries. Grabbing her Versace washbag, she headed to the bathroom to make herself ready for the world.

She paused as listened in at her mother's bedroom. Snuffling sounds emerged from behind the closed door.

"I'll give her another few minutes before it all kicks off" thought Rosie, and headed out of their flat, making for the shared bathroom accessed by Rosie, her mum, and the tenants in number 31a. Tenants. Plural. Rosie shivered. She entered the dark corridor that separated 31a and her flat, 31b. In truth, it was just one basement apartment, but it had been converted into two flats by a previous landlord. The only light came from a filthy window above the front door, 6 steps up from the corridor. A bare bulb hung forlornly between the flats, spreading dull shadows into all corners of the hall. She stood for a moment and listened. She could hear movement in 31a, indistinct against the caterwauling of the seagulls outside, screeching as they fought over last night's discarded chips that were a regular feature of Bognor's side-streets. Her mind drifted, caught between the flats; On one side the private world of her life with her mum. Opposite, the secret lives of her tenants and outside the seasonal ebb and flow of tourists. She stared out of the window above the door and briefly imagined herself a gull, soaring over the town. She took in the beach, the brown sea, the serried rows of Victorian housing, the post war expansion and then the glitzy new builds, all timber frame and New England styling. Like the rings of a fallen oak in nearby Hotham Park, Bognor's civic life could be chronicled by the changing architecture of the last 150 years. Sitting incongruously near the seafront were the white sails of the Butlin's Holiday Park. Bognor. Britain's sunniest town.

Slack-jawed Rosie stared out through the salt-and-grime encrusted transom window, long bereft of its colourful Victorian stained-glass features. Blank-eyed Rosie went to that place she often found herself, had always found herself as long as she could remember, neither dreaming nor a little death, just…absent. This place of comfort, of briefly not existing was rudely yanked from her by the sharp, metallic crack of the door of 31a opening, and the fleeting vision of Mr Jones, a dark blue paisley silk dressing gown covering his thin body passing before her and into the bathroom. The door slammed shut.

"Sod it' thought Rosie, as she leant against the door jamb and started to pick at her nails, completely unaware that her mother's money-making scheme was about to explode.

MR JONES

"*Every day I wake up I thank the Lord I'm Welsh*". Lying in bed I mouth the homage to my home country, my *Gwlad,* as sung by Cerys Matthews. Don't know what it is about being Welsh, but it's got something to do with knowing we're connected to our past, we Britons, to the original people of these Isles. Before the Anglo-Saxon invasion. Being Welsh is not being English. But here I am, an émigré washed up on the south coast of this *nook-shotten isle* in sunny' Bognor Regis. But not for long. Counting down the days, mate, counting down the days.

Damn but this flat smells. Smells bad. Smells of lonely old men, dying, alone and unloved beneath filthy sheets. How's that song go?

'The cigarette of a single man / Burns in the ashtray by his bed / He pulls the ring of another can / And holds it up beside his head / The book he reads is on the floor / He's read it several times before'

Great band, Squeeze. But I'm not lonely. I'm on the way up, up and out. Just getting ready to make my move, any day now. Get all my ducks in a row, not gonna end up a sitting duck. Gotta keep it all under control, Mikey boy. Nothing untoward. No mishaps, missteps, and no messing with the missus next door. She's trouble, is Rosie. A slattern my mother would've called her, with her rich Aberdawe vowels and her Chapel bile. God rest her soul. Now Mikey, there's the alarm, time to get going.

Check first. Chair, dressing gown, slippers, washbag, nothing moved. Check. Table, two chairs, exactly in the right position, nothing moved. Check. Briefcase. Christ alive. Unmoved. Check. Air vent…. from here in the dark, it looks as it always looks, it's just an air vent, right? Right. Traffic rumbling passed above my head. That Russian nightmare of a landlady could at least get the windows cleaned, put in new curtains. But she's a tight one, that Ludmilla, unlike Rosie. She's well loose, I reckon. She'd be a Valley girl back in Wales. Gotta use what you've got to get on in life. Me, it was maths. Accountancy is gunna take me to the top of the world.

Lying here, staring at the stained ceiling, makes me wonder how I ended up here. This is a shit room, in a shit house in a shit town. Bugger Bognor, never a truer word. When I first arrived I did my research, y'know, find out where I was living, immersed myself in a bit of local history. Turns out Bognor was pretty much a nowhere place from Saxon times, just smelling of fish and drunk smugglers. Then – get this – a hatter.... yes, a hatter, having holidayed here for several years in the late 18th century, decided it was a fine place for a resort. Tenby, that's a resort. Even Rhyl. But Bognor? What qualified a hatter to make this decision I have no idea; it was all just low-lying swamp. And the beach! Don't get me started. Feet-numbing shingle. That's not a beach, that's an exercise in extreme Reflexology. Delusions of grandeur I reckon, unless of course being a London hatter in 1784 was THE most Rock n Roll thing going, and he was absolutely minted. It's not exactly the med, is it! But he built himself a resort and it's been rotting slowly ever since. Then along comes Billy Butlin, a fairground hawker with – guess what – delusions of grandeur. Rumour has it that he wanted to build a holiday camp on the sandy beach at West Wittering. So appalled were the stuck-up locals at the thought of working-class people from 'Sarf London' clogging up the highways and byways that they clubbed together and blocked Butlin by buying all the land themselves. So now the village is a ghost town of weekenders down from Richmond. Even The Tatler said it was the place to have your second home. Strange they never recommended Bognor.

Still, I won't be here for much longer, I can guarantee you that! Just gotta keep my head down, be invisible, do my job and then I'm done. I'm gone with the wind, out like Flynn. Invisible and then untraceable. Not gunna make the mistakes I made last time. Rule one: Stay Away From Dodgy Casinos.

Shower first, don't break the routine, don't raise any suspicions, Mikey. Radio first. Who uses a cassette player these days? Soon I'll have a state-of-the-art system, controlled from every room in the house. Proper B&O. Who is that? Marsalis? "*Jazz is not dead; it just smells funny*". That's a classic Zappa line, that. But I don't mind it, see. That soprano sax keeps my thoughts at bay, it fills my mind so there's no room for the demons, the what if's. Damn my imagination!

Onward. Shower…. shit, eyes down, don't get caught with Rosie, and get in before her otherwise you'll be late. Can't be late. Boss would go mental. Made it.

LUDMILLA

The first struggle, a daily struggle in a life blighted by struggle, was to prise open her eyes. Most mornings came after evenings when drink had sent her to bed without first removing heavy layers of eyelash glue and expensive mascara. Ludmilla lay still and stretched all the muscles of her face, enjoying the cracking sensation. It reminded her of those far-away days of summer, her face salt-encrusted from too much time spent on Oleksandrivka beach, as the hot sun dried the Black Sea brine into sparkling crystals. And she loved the drive back home to the port of Kherson. She would stick her face out of the back window of the family Trabant and feel the warm wind flicking away the remaining moisture to leave her skin taught and prickly.

She was just drifting back off to sleep, the warm Ukrainian wind feathering her face, when her alarm jarred her back into the cold Bognor present. She sat up and switched off the insistent bleeping. With an extended foot she drew back the edge of the curtain and looked out into the pre-dawn sodium glow of Bognor

Regis. Bogbados. Bozch-Nor Du Roi. Kherson and Bognor were not that different, both having illustrious histories that could be glimpsed in the crumbling architecture, obscured by ubiquitous Buddleia that sprung from every crack in the decaying cement. Ludmilla sighed. To work.

She had just pulled on a pink toweling robe over her stout body when her daughter burst in.

"Do you bloody mind, girl!" she rasped. "Is not Piccadilly Circus, you knock, yes?"

"Alright mum...keep yer..." Rosie stopped herself as her mother turned away and adjusted her blonde wig. Just 16 when reactor No 4 at Chernobyl exploded, Ludmilla spent most of that summer playing blithely in the Dnieper River as it wound its way past Chernobyl, Kiev and down to the Black Sea port of Kherson. Simple alopecia wasn't good enough for Ludmilla. She needed a better story.

"E takes so bloody long in the morning, mum, drives me nuts. What's 'e doing in there, knocking one out I wouldn't be surprised"

"You a filthy mind, girl" said Ludmilla as she checked the damage to her face in the mirror.

"Yeah, well, learnt from the master, din' I" said Rosie. "Anyway, ain't you got something to say to me?"

"I have? What I do last night? Can't remember. Whatever. I apologise. There, now go".

"No, you daft sod. My birthday. 21ˢᵗ birthday, mum, you promised you'd take me up Chichester later, all them posh shops".

"'Course, Baboushka, I not forgotten. Get him sorted next door then we go. An' happy birthday. You got everything ready?"

"Yeah, but I'm grabbing a shower first. Hang on, I think 'e's done. Grab the post Mum".

Rosie disappeared into the corridor. Ludmilla thought for a moment. Was it really 21 years ago? She had been in a cavern bar near Kherson dock. Russian sailors, what was left of the Black Sea fleet, were in town for the new year were and looking for a party. She was out too, looking for a little cash and a good time. They had money in their pockets, and they yearned for female company. She was happy to drink their drinks, listen to their stories and when they were de-trousered in the alley upstairs, she deployed her secret weapon, a small canister of pepper spray. As they floundered about, cursing and wiping their eyes, she swiftly removed their wallet and scarpered. The evening had been going well, a large guy from Minsk was in his cups and in her bra. But as she heaved him to his feet her secret weapon spilled from her pocket and skittered away under several tables. She tried to pull away but Minsk-Man, strong from hauling anchor ropes, kept her close-hauled. By the time she realised she was pregnant he was in the murky depths off Sakhalin in a nuclear sub and she'd forgotten his name.

CHARLIE

Charlie enjoyed his job, temporary though it was. He could get out of the house early, do a round and get into Chichester Uni in time for the first dance class. Bognor wasn't his first choice. He would've preferred Arts Ed frankly, a better route to music theatre stardom. He was good enough. But his mum had persuaded him the south coast would be a great option, with his Nan so close. But then she had died, and life suddenly got complicated. Charlie didn't like complicated. He liked simple.

His red post-bag bouncing on his hips, he took a couple of steps from number 33 Torrance Avenue to number 31. Two doors, one for the main house, and one that led down 6 steps to 2 flats. His mail for the basement flats consisted mostly of flyers and unsolicited garbage, but he was under strict instructions from the mad Russian landlady in 31b, so he reached for the door. From nowhere, a dog leapt out and grabbed his trouser leg and tried to pull him away. Must've been lying on the ground in front of the street-level window. It was hard keeping a track of the whereabouts of the various Bognor dogs that blighted his round.

"Bugger off, you mad pooch, g'wan…" He flicked his foot and caught the dog under its chin. The dog let go momentarily, allowing Charlie time to dash into the basement flat. He shut the door quickly lest the dog came back for seconds. At the top of the stairs, Charlie paused. With his one free hand he quickly checked the state of his afro. Not a full on 70's Black Panther job, more of a premiership footballer style, with a subtle fade up from the temples, courtesy of the Harry, the Kurdish barber on the high street.

Previous visits to number 31 had led to him feeling he was in with a chance with Rosie. Nothing serious, obviously, but a welcome distraction from the intense conversations he found himself embroiled in with the women on the Music Theatre degree. He was a 3rd year student, aiming for the West End, maybe 'Hamilton' one day, but he needed the postman job to avoid the debts. There was only so much blather he could take about race and gender. Sometimes a man just needed an honest shag. Uncomplicated. Rosie seemed like she might be willing.

With the post for 31a and 31b in his hands he knocked at 31b. Just then he heard the door to the bathroom go behind him. He spun round, only to see the shady Mr Jones flit across into his flat, slamming his door. Simultaneously the door to 31b opened and Rosie barged passed him, trailing a heady scent of sweat and Lancome, disappearing into the bathroom and slamming the door.

"Rosie…" was all he managed to get out before he felt a sharp tap on his shoulder. Turning back he was confronted with a close-up of Ludmilla.

"Charlie boy, so good to see you, what you got in your bag for me today, eh?" Ludmilla chuckled throatily. "Let me see the contents of your sack, yes!"

So close was Charlie to Ludmilla that he was momentarily overcome by her garlicky vodka breath and the realisation that every part of her face was covered in some kind of glamour product.

"I.…er.… just some…"

"Give me post for 31a, yes? As agreed," muttered Ludmilla, snatching the post from his hand. He was about to remonstrate but she was gone. Another door slammed. Charlie hovered for a moment, waiting for Rosie to make an appearance, though getting so close to the mother had not imbued him with enthusiasm for further encounters. He recalled the words of his father, Dexter Skank, rhythm guitarist with the London Ska band The Skankers.

"You wanna look at the mother before you commit yerself, son. 'Specially white girls, right, cos the sun does terrible things to 'em. Not like us lions of Africa. Black don't crack. And look at their arse. That's where a young girl's arse is going in 20 year's time. Remember that." Fabulously of his times, his dad. No doubt the women on his Uni course would have him cancelled. Chastened, for the time being, Charlie hurried onto the street, pausing only to hand the dog a special delivery of a sharp kick.

WHAT THE DOG SAW.

Returning to his post, lying against the pavement-height window, Dog watched the postman disappear along the road. Dog ran his tongue along the gums of his lower jaw. No blood. No damage. He rested his head on his front paws and peered in through the dirty window. The Nice Man wasn't home yet, but he would be soon. For now, though, the other man was inside. Dressed now in a suit that had once been smart, the Thin Man was pacing about his room, checking his briefcase, turning off the radio, straightening his pictures on the wall. Every picture was of a car – not the type you'd see in Bognor normally. These cars were flash, bright colours and sleek outlines, with fancy Italian-sounding names. Dog recognised one of the cars, his old master had one the same. Dog briefly pined for a distant past, when he lived in a big house on the Aldwick Bay Estate. His master was a big man, always dressed in black with lots of gold jewellery, took him up to London on many occasions. Oh, the smells of London!

Then one day a new dog appeared. Enormous, black, with huge teeth. Dog was by no means small. He could take care of himself, but this new canine destroyer – he was a different breed altogether. His master started walking around Bognor with this dog, this interloper, on a very short but powerful leather lead. He sensed his master was not happy, seemed nervous. He could smell that, through the lotions and potions the man splashed all over himself every morning, scents to hide the underlying stench of fear and violence. His descent from pampered pooch to street hound was swift, unexplained, and unexpected. He woke one morning, and the house was empty. Stayed empty for days. Then men arrived, turfed him out, locked the doors and went away. Now someone else lives in his house – well, lived but they were never there. DFL's. Down From London when the weather suits. He never saw his master – or the black dog ever again. He hung around for a while, but one day, he was sniffing around the grounds when he picked up a scent, a familiar tang of expensive oils and perfumes. Something else mixed in there too, something…. edible. He snuffled around, found the source by a large oak tree, and started to dig. It wasn't deep, but he knew what it was. He stopped his digging and turned away and never came back. But hunger drove him along the beach, from bin to bin, until a friendly bloke with a funny smile started feeding him scraps. For some reason he wasn't allowed into this man's house, so he had taken to sleeping outside against the window.

Dog observed the human behaviour through the grimy window and thought something wasn't right. Something was afoot. He could sense that. Dog sense. With a vastly superior olfactory ability coupled with an acute sense of his surroundings and with his reptilian brain in full flow, this dog knew things the humans inside the house could never even get close to realising. A horse can detect a human's heart rate and breathing at 10 metres. A dog can smell a human corpse 30 metres underwater. Animals can use their brains in ways humans have long forgotten.

The Thin Man swung the door open and met the young woman in the corridor, still in her night wear, loosely tied. Dog observed how the man seemed keen to avoid the young woman – his heart rate, normally high, seemed even higher and his breathing quickened. The young woman let the Thin Man go, and the door shut. Dog knew what was about to happen. It happened very day at this time, so he got ready, got his claws out and bared his fangs.

The Thin Man exited the house at speed, slamming the door behind him. Dog flew at him, this boney streak of nervous piss who lived where the other man lived, the Nice Man. Every day Dog tried to chase Thin

Man away, and today was no different. Snarling, he threw himself at the man's shins, grabbed a mouthful of trouser fabric and shook it rapidly. The Wolf in the Dog seared through his blood, the fight was on, his hackles were up and there'd be only one victor. The same victor, every day. Thin Man swung his briefcase, catching a glancing blow on Dog's shoulder before a large Bus appeared on the scene and Thin Man stepped on, shaking himself free of the dog.

Dog, quite satisfied, went back to watch the unfolding spectacle in the flat, wondering, ever hopeful, that today would be the day that Thin Man never re-appeared.

ROSIE

"MUM! E's gone!"

The door to 31b flew open and Ludmilla appeared, dragging behind her a large cart piled high with bedding and other belongings.

"Take the keys, Rosie" panted the older woman, as she drew up outside 31a. Rosie unlocked 31a and threw open the door.

"Christ he dun 'arf stink" she exclaimed. "Filthy beasts, men. Single men stink the worst 'n' all." She wafted the door back and forth a few times in a vain attempt to dispel the manly odour.

"I agree, daughter, but we have a job to do. Move!"

"Alright, alright. Giz the camera."

Ludmilla passed Rosie a smart Polaroid camera from the top of the cart. Rosie took several shots of the room and paced about impatiently shaking them dry.

"Where we going then?" she asked.

"For what?"

"For my birthday you tight-fisted old hag. 21 is important, you know, I should be having a right bash with all me mates"

"Ach, maybe you go Sheiks tonight with your chavvy friends and get blind drunk. Maybe you strike lucky and get kneetrembler under the pier. Who knows?"

"Really mum? I'm not a Bognor Dog. I got aspirations. Gunna have me own salon."

"Well, your salon needs financing, so you need to raise capital. Which is what we do here, no? We scrimp, save, and then we invest. But don't worry, we not go Chichester. Special treat, we go Portsmouth."

"Gunwharf! The outlet centre of the south coast! Aw, that's amazing, Mum!"

"They dry yet?"

Rosie checked the two pictures and stuffed them inside the left side of her bra, then felt around inside the right cup for something she couldn't quite locate.

"Christ, your tits like 2lbs of shit in a 1lb bag," laughed her mum.

"You can talk…got them."

Rosie pulled out two other crumpled Polaroids, lay them onto the table and the women bent over and observed them like museum curators examining Abyssinian scrolls.

"His mess is as usual. Don't think he'd notice if anything was out of place," said Rosie.

"No, we do this properly. Get going."

The two women now entered a well-rehearsed drill, stripping the room of every identifiable personal effect of Mr Mike Jones and piling them in the middle. Once the room was stripped, they started unloading the cart, referring occasionally to the pictures on the table. They moved swiftly, fleet of foot and nimble-fingered. The effect was like watching a tightly choreographed ballet, as they dipped, swooped, threw objects from one another, slowly turning the room from Mr Jones' austere bachelor's pad into something much more chaotic, random, and very, very messy. Pictures of fast cars were exchanged for a few bucolic scenes and a faded photograph. A cassette was inserted into the cassette player. Mr Jones' grey duvet was replaced by garish, patterned bedding one would normally see in a child's room. A few clothes were randomly spread about the floor, some uneaten food left on the table. But there was nothing random about it. The two women checked and double- checked the placement of every item against the two Polaroids on the table.

The smooth-running operation shuddered to a halt when the dog outside let out an excited howl, his wagging tail unwittingly beating out a warning signal against the pane of glass, alerting the two women to impending disaster.

"Are you shitting me?!" exclaimed Rosie

"He is early, maybe the bus delayed, got an earlier one. Hurry, girl."

The two women went into overdrive, piling Mr Jones's belongings into the cart, careening out of the door, just as the front door opened. Luckily for them the new arrival was busy making a huge fuss of the dog, so he missed Ludmilla disappearing into 31b with the cart and Rosie trying to lock the door of 31a, fumbling and dropping the keys. She snatched them up and bolted for the safety of her flat, slamming the door behind her. Flat 31a was now transformed into a completely different person's flat.

Into that flat walked a night watchman called Joe.

Joe had no idea he was sharing a flat with Mr Jones.

Mr Jones didn't know the man called Joe existed.

Ludmilla and Rosie's deception afforded them double rent from the same flat. It was not without its dangers. The trolley now stowed ready for the evening change, the two women stood and go their breath back.

"Fuck, mum, that was close. We need a warning system."

"Ah, no bother, we made it – we always make it. The man is a *pridurok*, which is a great help. Now, store the new pictures please."

"Noooooo!!!" said Rosie, slapping her hand against her forehead.

"What what what, what you done now, huh?"

"I've only gone an' left the new pictures on the table"

"*Shluha vokzal'naja*" gasped Ludmilla. "Idiot. Go back in there and get them. Now!"

"How, though, mum?"

"You should've thought of that before you a silly cow. Go!"

SLOW JOE

WEST SUSSEX POLICE, BOGNOR DIVISION:

INVESTIGATION INTO THE UNEXPLAINED DEATH OF JOE NOWAK, otherwise known as 'Slow Joe'. Report compiled from witnesses, information provided by family members through telephone conversations, texts and WhatsApp messages.

2nd November.

According to the CCTV record and his manager's statement, Joe Nowak left his workplace, A1 Warehousing Solutions at 7.30am having finished his shift as night watchman. Joe, by all accounts was an odd fellow, very amiable and happy, though according to his manager, Aparna Singh, he was "like a 40-watt light bulb at midnight". (*PC Ricketts note: I think she meant he was a bit dim*). He arrived home by bus at 8.12am and, according to Mrs Watson of 32 Torrance Avenue, he met and interacted with a stray dog outside his basement flat 31a Torrance Avenue. A few moments earlier another man departed the flat, who we can now identify as Michael Jones, also of Flat 31a, Torrance Avenue, who boarded the number 600 bus after an aggressive altercation with the said canine. Mr Jones was dressed in a dark suit for work and carried a small attaché-style briefcase.

NOTE: Mrs Watson has been a very useful source of information regarding this case, though PC Ricketts felt she spent most of her day just staring across at Number 31 on the off chance of discovering salacious or incriminating evidence against the landlady and owner or the basement apartment, Ludmilla Shatalova, in the hope of having her deported. Shatalova is her actual surname – it has come to our attention that the London Road Police Station in Bognor Regis keeps a 'Top Ten' of inappropriate Eastern European surnames and 'Shatalova' is currently number 1. Top Brass are concerned about the racist overtones of this league and recommends the CC move to close down this practice.

According to family statements, Joe's emigration to Bognor Regis needs some explaining, and has some bearing on how he lived his life. Joe grew up on a farm near the Polish village of Checiny. Joe was born with an unidentified skull deformity, leading to his nickname, '*Glowa Fasoli*', or 'Bean Head'. His mother had died giving birth to him and his father, grief-stricken, had got blind drunk and fell into the canal and drowned. Joe had an older sister, Lucy, who was now looked after by her aunt, but there wasn't room in the house for Joe. He was therefore adopted by a local farmer, who saw him as possible free labour later in life. The farmer, Andrei Drab was an unpleasant man with an unpleasant family, but Joe managed to grow up a happy – if none too bright – young man. He had a tight circle of good friends, but he was inappropriately smitten by his stepsister, Magdalena Drab, the village beauty. Joe also had 4 stepbrothers who, by all accounts, amounted to the 'local mafia', each one a tall, blond Adonis, referred to as the Checiny Greek Gods. In a shocking turn of events, Magdalena, after years of ignoring Joe around the house, suddenly decided to marry him in a rushed wedding service held at the local church. The marriage was short-lived and precipitated Joe's departure from the village, from Poland, and his arrival in the UK. Anecdotal evidence suggests that on the first morning of married life Joe was attacked by all four brothers and threatened with death unless he left. It later transpired that Magdalena hated her brothers and father so vehemently that she married the obviously physically inferior Joe just to spite them. Joe was heartbroken by these events and disappeared the next day, before contacting his family, having arrived in Bognor Regis, a town with a sizeable Polish population.

Joe was a creature of habit and found great solace in the presence of animals, with whom he felt a natural affinity. The landlady of his flat, 31a Torrance Road had a blanket ban on the keeping of pets, but Joe found ways around this rule.

According to his sister Lucy, on arriving home on the morning of the 2nd of November, and after entering his flat, his first concern would have been to feed a small colony of mice he had nurtured beneath the floorboards, using crumbs left over from his packed meal he took to work each evening. He later reported to his family that on this particular day, as he was crouching down behind the table, and having prised back a loose board, he heard his door open. Quickly returning the floorboard, fearing discovery, he stood to find Rosie Shatalova, the 21year old daughter of Landlady Ludmilla Shatalova in his room, standing right at the table. Both parties were shocked to see each other, and Joe thought he detected an air of guilt about Rosie as she seemed to be hiding something behind her back. It was clear to Joe's family that history was repeating itself, and that Joe was very smitten by the very inappropriate Rosie Shatalova, who by all accounts, and according to several of the male officers at the London St branch, whilst attractive to look at, had a somewhat tarnished reputation.

The awkward moment between Joe and Rosie, and an explanation of exactly why she had let herself into his room was broken by the arrival of Ludmilla Shatalova with the rent book. Joe told Lucy he was confused, thinking he was up to date with his rent, but Mrs Shatalova assured him he was in arrears and took all the cash he had on him. Joe tried to make conversation with Rosie, but the Shatalovas left as soon as they had his money.

Mrs Watson observed the street level window open, and the dog jumped through into the flat. Lucy reported that he played with the dog every evening, fed it scraps but struggled to keep the dog quiet, fearing discovery by the formidable Ludmilla Shatalova. Lucy reported that Joe, whilst grateful for the flat, lived in fear of Mrs Shatalova, and did everything he could do avoid her displeasure. After about 10 minutes the window opened, and the dog leapt out and took off towards Hotham Park.

The next part of Joe's routine is of vital importance and was only told to the Polish Interpol authorities under great duress by Lucy and several other members of her family. Joe was a simple soul, easily influenced, and had, several months previously, purchased a pet snake from an unscrupulous colleague at the Warehouse. Told it was rare and very dangerous, and thus of great value, Joe was persuaded that the snake needed a good home to go to and would be very content with a regular diet of mice. Toxicology results have confirmed that the snake was in fact an 'Inland Taipan', illegally imported from Australia.

An extract from Joe Nowak phone conversation as remembered by his sister Lucy.
".... it was a strange morning, really. I dunno, Lucy, I think she likes me, I mean, why did she sneak into my room like that? Then her mum bursts in as if to catch us out or something, but she says I still owed her rent, which is funny cos I thought I paid last week. Lucky I had some cash, not that I go out and have anything to spend it on. So, I did all my usual stuff, y'know, played with Freddie. That's the dog. Pat needed a feed.... I know, Pat is not a great name for a snake, but honestly, every time I look at him, I just hear 'Pat'. I think about patting him like a dog. Not a good idea. I should call him Christof after Magdalena's horrible older brother, but I don't want to be reminded.
The mice colony is coming along nicely, they're breeding well. They're so tame now so I just coax one out

and dispatch him – or her - with a swift knock to the table. I suppose I should be cross and glad about Ludmilla that she doesn't clean very well. My ritual of feeding Pat starts with the music. Puts me in the mood I suppose, it's a bit exotic. Found a tape at the Sue Ryder shop of Indian Tunes, and one of the pieces reminds me of snake-charmer music. Wailing pipes. So, I put that on the cassette player. Dragged Pat's .... what they called, glass cage thing? Vivarium? Anyhoo, seems to be safe under the bed, so dragged it out and put it onto the bed. I've got this special glove from Amazon, it's like a medieval knight's gauntlet, wire mesh job, just gives some protection against a nip from those fangs. Dave said it was very venomous so I must be careful. So I put the glove on, remove the lid, dangle the mouse over the top cos I wants to see him, otherwise, y'know, what's the point? He rises slowly from under these dried up leaves I got from the park, he snatches the mouse, swallows it whole and flops back down. That's it. Bit of a dead loss as a pet frankly, Luce, and I'm not sure why I've got him, but Dave was very insistent, and at only £400 he said it was a bargain. So yeah, put him back, had a pot noodle for, well, I call it dinner but it's 9 o'clock in the morning and here we are. I'm off to bed now. Going out? You know I haven't got any friends Lucy. I can't speak English really, so I only use the Polish shops. Did I tell you about the nightclub on the pier? It's called 'Sheiks', it's like something out of Hollywood, it's so glamorous. Dave took

*me there once, on a night off, we met these girls, right,
really glamorous, and I liked them a lot but Dave called
them Bognor Dogs, which I didn't understand, especially
as he disappeared later saying he was taking one of the dogs
for a walk.... (end of relevant transmission).*

LUDMILLA

Ludmilla, realising Rosie might blow the whole double-rent deception with her carelessness grabbed the rent-book and made good the excuse to be in 31a without invitation. Joe was weak, and Ludmilla was an expert in recognising and manipulating weak men. She got a second helping of rent from him, which was a bonus, especially as she had clean forgotten about Rosie's birthday, and was now committed to a shopping spree to Gunwharf. She should've thought quicker and offered her Worthing instead. But as factory outlets go, there were high-end brand label bargains to be had.

Back in the flat the two women prepared for the day's shopping and troughing. They shared a mirror, make-up, and plans.

"So mum, whatcha planning for me birthday then? Shopping, a boozy lunch, more shopping then home?"

"Ach, do you need more clothes, babes? How about a nice walk along Little'ampton beach?"

"Christ no, Mum! LA is no day out unless you're on day release from Ford Prison!"

"Well, we have to be back for the evening turnaround, you know, no messing, like clockwork, every day. Pass me that mascara."

"For how long, Mum? Gets so tedious, never a day off. I wanna live my life…."

"Enough, you know nothing, your life is nothing if you have no money, yes? And if no money then you mus' have man, rich man, to have and to hold until you divorce, with big pay day. But we live in bloody Bognor so only rich men are dodgy London gangster, yes? They see girl like you, big tits, Loboutins and Armani, tight dress, they want you. For that we need money, so we fleece these *debily*. Pass me the concealer."

"I'm not after a man, Mum, I wanna start me own business. Nails, lashes, fillers, it'll be great. We can do home visits and everyfink."

"Whatefer, you dream you dreams my girl but still we turn the flat around twice daily and we take double rent from Mr Jones and Mr Nowak. Ride the wild tiger, my uncle used to say"

"Did you?"

"Did I what?"

"Ride his wild tiger?"

"Ach, it was a mangy thing, he shot it when it became too expensive to feed. Got nice new bear for circus. Proper Russian bear."

"Well I ain't spending all my time servicing these two bollocks".

"Rosie, you keep in perspective, yes? It's maximum 20 minutes a day, twice 10 minutes and we're done, we get on with our lives. For that we get rent as if we own two flats. And rent is high, no? Slow Joe, he knows nothing, he just grateful for a roof, doesn't realise he pays too much. And Mr Jones…well, he's a strange one. Accountant, he said, but he didn't blink when I told him rent for smelly basement flat. All he wants to know is does air vent work. I say no, he takes the flat. I think maybe he a serial killer".

"Nah…how do me eyes look?…. I reckon he's just a lonely sod. Sometimes I look at him and I think… maybe… 10 years younger, I probably would have, y'know."

"No, Rosie, you save yourself for rich man. 'Cos you're worth it!"

Both women cackled and finished their preparations in a flurry of powder and scent. After much discussion about suitable shoes for the expedition, the appropriate handbag and other accessories, they were done. They tiptoed past 31a, bending theatrically to listen at the door, stifling their giggles.

"Fast asleep already, sad bugger" said Rosie.

It was 9.30am on a mild November morning when Ludmilla and Rosie finally emerged, like exotic insects from their burrows, teetering on their heels as if newly born, towards the number 700 bus stop.

Meanwhile, across town, Mike Jones descended from the number 600 bus, sweating profusely in the autumn breeze.

MR JONES

"Bad journey, went inside my head too much, got spooked. Starting to see things, people, thought I was being followed. Get yer breath back, boyo, wipe the sweat away, don't give her any reason to be suspicious. Here we are, front door, "Gold Property Development" on a small brass plaque. As if. Give the signal knock, 'ti tat, ti tat, ti tat'. Spyhole darkens – that'll be Milo checking. Bolts drawn, chains rattled, door swings and we're in. Milo stands before me. Absolute gorilla. 6'4" at least, muscled, chiselled, tight-fitting black suit, white shirt, and the ominous bulge of a Beretta in a holster. Probably the 92FS. Style and tradition mixing carbon and walnut. Tasty. For all that, he's always very friendly. Guess that's what makes him so terrifying.

"Morning Milo, are we well?

"We are indeed Mr Jones. Punctual as ever."

"Of course. Personally, I'd never trust an accountant who can't get to work on time. Profit and loss, acceptable risk, it's very much like getting the bus. Hold-ups, breakdowns, burst water mains God forbid…is she in?"

"She'll be in presently. Expect her to visit mid-morning."

With that, Milo turns away into the guts of the house, various rooms, doors behind which God knows what happens. I occasionally have a snapshot through an open door of people in white overalls unpacking boxes of product, stacking them up, ready to cut, re-cut, re-packaged, and re-distributed. Classic middle-man operation making all the big bucks. I should know. My job is to account for all the ins and outs, notate by hand in a green bound ledger the 10's and the 100's right up to the 1,000,000's. This unassuming between-the-wars faux Arts and Crafts mansion is the hub for all cocaine and heroin distribution for the south coast of the UK. We're talking Brighton, Portsmouth, Southampton, Worthing. Yeah, and Bognor! All those Media types camping out in Lewes get their nose candy from here. Scumbags with dogs on ropes in Brighton night shelters, party girls and off-duty sailors' home from Belize in the puke-stained streets of Portsmouth. The posh Londoners in their weekend homes in the Witterings and all their mates down for some sun, sea, and recreational drugs. All the Uni kids getting high on Student Finance England, all connected like a spider's web to this pad in Middleton-on-sea. And at the centre of the web sits Lulu Gold. An absolute, down-the-line psychopath. If she was a stick of Bognor rock she'd have 'Psycho' written right through her. Don't be deceived by the sticky pink outer layer. This sweetie will rot your brain and fill you full of cavities.

Right, to my office.

It's a fairly average 1930's seaside mansion, but the inside has been ripped out and seriously pimped. I mean, what else does she do with the money? Never known her to take a break. The car isn't flash, though apparently it's totally secure, you know, bullet proof and that. So the floor – Italian marble, the finest in Swedish hand-made furniture, hand-printed wallpaper from De Gournay and the de rigeur vast fish tank that will be the first casualty in any future shoot-out, no doubt. Draped around the property like extras from *Reservoir Dogs* were the Men in Black. Mini-Milo's to a man, provenance unknown. Do they pop into this world as fully formed henchmen from central casting? How do they stay so fit when all they seem to do is sit around all day? Haven't they got homes to go to?

I walk past all the men like a white mouse walking around a cattery. All eyes on me. My office is on the first floor, unassuming and windowless. Maybe to stop prying eyes. There's a huge safe built into the wall behind my desk, so people are in and out, making large deposits and occasionally taking small amounts away, for bribes, for payments I don't want to think about. They go into the 'Misc' column.

Couple of curiosities. The safe is old fashioned, no biometric entry or anything like that. Just numbers and a big handle. And my books. No computers, no storage, no iCloud. Just the finest quality German Ledgers, imported from Berlin. Don't ask me why. I suspect because Lulu Gold is not a techie kind of person, doesn't want clever people hiding things from her, she wouldn't want anything explained to her, you know. In fact, if she ever says 'Can you explain that to me' then you know you're in trouble.

Sitting at my desk - large, vintage, green-baized top, I can feel the safe behind me. I've checked – bought equipment from Amazon – there are no cameras in here. So, at some point today, I'll do what I've done virtually every day for the last two years. I'll open the safe, take out a small wedge of untraceable cash and put it into my briefcase. I'll get creative with the pencil and rubber and 'Hey Presto'....it never existed. Except that it does. And it's all mine. Hidden in the flat. So now you know why I sweat."

LULU GOLD

The black Jag with tinted windows pulled up outside number 14 Marine Terrace. Nothing happened for a moment. Then the house door opened, and Milo skipped down the steps like Ray Liotta in 'Goodfellas'. With practiced grace he swung back the car door and nodded with deference to the sole occupant, other than Skunk, the driver. A pair of Sabine Flat Jimmy Choo's swung out first, followed by the long legs of Lulu Gold. Tall, with a willowy grace, her clothes hung on her like a catwalk model. A phone was clamped to her ear, and she wore shades, oblivious to the incongruity of wearing sunglasses in November in Bognor Regis. Nobody got to look Lulu Jones in the eye.

"I don't care what he said, get it done" said Lulu tersely into the phone then handed it to Milo and continued into the house. Her skin was rich Ghanian brown, her hair platinum white, cut to a severe bob. Her full lips were painted a shocking blood red. Her hands seemed large and thin and were covered in tight leather gloves.

All she had to do was walk. Every door opened before her, chairs pulled back, pushed in, drinks appeared, and a thin black cheroot placed into her hand and lit. Walk and breathe. Everything else was taken care of. This was a woman very much in charge of her environment. Right now, she was sitting in her office, attended by Milo. She motioned to him to sit with her. The chairs were original Jacobsen Swan chairs in red leather. She had to spend the money on something.

Milo waited as Jones swilled ice round a tumbler of Glenmorangie. She sipped demurely and dragged on the cheroot, threw her head back, pursed her lips and exhaled a long, slow thin line of smoke.

"Good weekend, Milo?" she inquired in a voice that was controlled, smooth and accent-less.

"Very pleasant, ma'am. Took the boat up the river, fished a bit, a few beers…"

Jones drank and smoked. Milo watched. Both had secrets as bleak as the human mind could create, and in the face of such knowledge, long and empty silences were a comfort and a refuge.

"I tried fishing once," said Jones. "It didn't suit. Seemed so pointless. Sitting for hours, thinking nothing. It's what fishmongers are for."

"That's the draw, Miss Gold, the nothingness," said Milo.

"Yes, you men. You like to go to your nothing brain. Me, I don't stop thinking. Never, not a heartbeat. That's why I am so mind-bogglingly successful," said Gold, taking another drag, her voice neither raised nor hushed, just…there. Milo smiled.

Behind every great woman is a story worth telling, because it's a man's world, and successful and powerful women are few and far between. Some great women ape their male counterparts and others trade on their femininity. The lucky few get their by

just being themselves. Lulu Gold became a powerful
and immensely rich dealer in drugs by confounding
men's expectations of how women behave without
ever losing the profound qualities that make women so
much more powerful than men, if only they realised it.
She built loyalty by caring and nurturing, and repaid
disloyalty with a dispassionate cruelty that left strong
men gagging into the gutter. Her punishments were
rarely brutal or swift, but slow and so psychologically
screwed up that lucky survivors were mesmerised like
rodents before a snake. The images and experiences
of her victims, of their families and loved ones were
seared into the neural pathways of all that worked for
her, engendering both a fierce and terrified loyalty but
also a manic respect. Nowadays she very rarely had to
access the dark that lived inside her. That job was done.
She had arrived at a consensus with those around her.
She was queen of all she surveyed. And yet....

The phone on the low table between them vibrated.
Milo answered, listened silently, then handed it to
Lulu. She, too, listened, taking a small mouthful of
whisky, and letting it swirl about her pristine teeth.
Then she spoke, her voice quiet, low and menacing.
The conversation finished, she switched off the phone
and returned it to the table. With an imperceptible nod
of her head Milo was dismissed. He stood and left the
room, a smirk of pleasure spreading across his face. He

was about to do what he liked doing best. He called a few of the minor gorillas to his side and they left the building and roared off in the black Jag. And with that, Lulu Gold relaxed. She sat back in her beautifully designed chair and enjoyed the rest of the cheroot, blowing smoke rings into the high ceiling and looking out over the English Channel from her office. Her eyes drifted around the room and settled on a small gilt-framed photograph. Black and white, from another era, two faces peered out from the past, one black, one white. Their cheeks were touching, their smiles wide, eye's a-sparkle. She kept the picture to remind her of where she came from.

How did she get here? Maybe a druggy mother, probably a prostitute, a victim of male violence witnessed nightly by a terrified child through the cracks in the door of the crack-den that she called home. Maybe one night the door burst open, and the young Lulu finds herself confronted by a tumescent and stoned beast of a man. Behind him the child can see the bloodied corpse of her mother. The man grabs the child, pins her down, when suddenly......

Lulu's story was not written by a gritty BBC Drama writer from Manchester. Lulu Jones was brought up in a loving house with a father who was a dentist and a mother who ran a successful Interior Design business. Sadly, for this happy couple, their only child was an utter psychopath. They spoilt her rotten, turned her into a Princess and gave her few boundaries. This approach to parenting did as much damage as the imagined abusive childhood. The final push, the tipping point that cemented her mania was when, thinking to give her the best start in life, they packed her off at an early age to a very expensive boarding school, thus ensuring that she would be well and truly fucked up for the rest of her life. Having no emotional hinterland due to such a stunted start in life, what she lacked in empathy she made up in narcissism. The world was hers for the plucking, and every man and woman merely players on her private stage.

But still she felt a soupcon of guilt when she saw the picture of her parents. But they had grown inquisitive, disapproving, mentioned the authorities. One weekend out hiking, they exited this life, pursued by a bear. At least that was the verdict.

She walked through the house, her goons snapping to attentiveness as they approached. Card games immediately abandoned; magazines dropped. Only one man didn't move. She stopped at his side.

"Nosmo, what the hell are you reading?" she asked.

Nosmo looked up from his book. Unremarkable to glance at, he had a quiet and menacing aura that came from his controlled eye contact that seemed to suggest a fury with the world. He was dressed in regulation black suit, single breasted, with a white shirt and black tie. His jacket bulged slightly from a concealed weapon. They locked eyes, an odd and strangely erotic silence held between them.

"Crime and Punishment, Ma'am. Very edifying."

"Hmm. Follow me, I want to have a word with our accountant." She broke the moment and walked off. Nosmo put down his book, having first bent over the top right corner of the page, stood from the chair in the corridor where he sat, straightened his jacket, and followed Lulu Gold up the stairs.

MR JONES

"I felt the air shift. She's here. The molecules of the oxygen in the house intermingle with some unknown element that is pure terror. She's walking up the stairs. There'll be no knock, she'll just walk straight in. It is her house after all. The door opens.

"Morning Mr Jones, I trust you are well."

"Never better, Miss Gold, never better."

"Excellent. Running totals please."

I open the ledger in front of me and spin it in her direction. Her leather gloves creak as she picked it up. Deputy Dawg Nosmo has silently padded into the room. I stare at him. He oozes mistrust. If there was an HR department I'd want him removed at the next performance review. Miss Gold is flicking through the pages. She looks across at Nosmo and raises an eyebrow a pencil width.

"Are these final, Mr Jones?" she asks me. I might wet myself.

"No no, just a preliminary trawl, Miss Gold. I'll do a full audit next week when everybody's figures are in."

"Good. Because you've miscalculated here...." She drops the book in front of me. "Column six, there. That should read 240, 000. Not 24,000."

"Ah! You're right, just a slip of a 'nought'." I grab my rubber and erase the offending figure and replace with the new one. Stop shaking, hand!

"Otherwise, it all seems in order. How much have we on site now?"

"Oh.... heavens, Miss Gold...precisely?"

"Precisely, Mr Jones, I'm not paying you for approximately. Your books say, what is it...Six million, nine hundred and thirty-two thousand, six hundred and fifty-two precisely. Wouldn't you say?"

I managed a whimpered 'Yes".

"Well, it's too much, we'll need to shift it next week. Nosmo, get that organised, will you? The Itchenor property is ready, I hear, the boys are all sorted for phase two. The family have got nowhere with the lawyers - unsurprisingly."

She smirks and Nosmo does what passes for a laugh. Unsettling. I'm not party to the 'Property' side of the business but I can't imagine for a moment it's legal, kosher, or whatever.

Lulu Gold places a large hand on my shoulder. She leans down and whispers into my ear. The smell of whisky, cheroot, and incredibly expensive perfume, plus the brush of a breast against my shoulder sends blood rushing to delicate extremities.

"I'm sure you'll be happier without that pile of temptation behind you, Mr Jones, eh? If there's one thing history has taught us, it's that whenever an organisation like mine is brought low by PC Plod or some governmental pen-pusher, it is invariably because of the duplicitous actions of the accountant. Never forget that." She squeezes my shoulder and I swear I hear a bone crack. Next thing, she's left the room. Nosmo lingers for a moment, staring intently at me, then he too turns and leaves. I pick up the waste-paper basket and throw up breakfast. I then consider knocking one out quickly to relive the pressure. Only joking.

I spend the rest of the day pondering one simple question.... does she know?

PART TWO

*"A secret's worth depends on
the people from whom it
must be kept."*

— Carlos Ruiz Zafón,

NOVEMBER 2, AFTERNOON

CHARLIE

His round finished, Charlie grabbed a coffee and a breakfast panini and just made class. He regretted the panini five minutes into a particularly upbeat routine from 'Hamilton' and was under-par in the singing class that followed. He had a lot on his mind, and he considered going to see Student Services for a chat over lunch, but an email plopped onto his phone that shook him up.

His Nan had died 6 months earlier, leaving her nondescript bungalow to her daughter, Suzy, Charlie's mum. Nan was old school, didn't like the fact that her Roedean-educated daughter had married a Jamaican musician – she softened when Dexter started earning more than the doctor Nan had imagined Suzy would marry. The bungalow might have been rather run-of-the-mill, but hey, it's location, location, location!

Itchenor is the most expensive village in the UK, a sailing community on Chichester Harbour, home to old and new money, rubbing shoulder to shoulder and sharing Buoys and occasionally partners on the weekends they manage to get down to Sussex from Richmond or Virginia Water.

Then the unthinkable happened. Before the family could take over the house, before Nan had even been buried in the small churchyard at Itchenor church, squatters had moved into the Bungalow. They had boarded themselves in very effectively, and when Charlie had tried to remonstrate with them, they threatened violence. Lawyers were hired, but they seemed to move so slowly, and on his few visits, Charlie was perturbed to hear hammering, grinding and other sounds of destruction coming from the house. What were they doing?

And now this. An email from the useless lawyer stating that the squatters had suddenly, miraculously, disappeared. The front door was wide open, hanging off its hinges. The local Estate Agents had made a quick inspection of the property, and it now pained him to have to report to the family that the lovely, 1930's bungalow with many original features, expected to fetch more than £800,000, was now little more than a shell. The inside had been totally ripped out. It was structurally unsound. They'd probably have to demolish it. The agents said they had a buyer offering £250,000 cash for it.

Charlie sat on a bench outside the Uni cafeteria and stared at the email. The cold, blunt legalese crashed against the huge emotion he was now feeling. Mum had promised him a windfall from the sale that would see him wipe out his student loan and mean he could concentrate on his studies and not have to be a Postman anymore. Any thoughts of handing in his notice had been cruelly taken away from him.

SLOW JOE

WEST SUSSEX POLICE, BOGNOR DIVISION: INVESTIGATION INTO THE UNEXPLAINED DEATH OF JOE NOWAK.
Extract from a phone conversation as recalled by his sister around 5pm GMT, 2nd November. May give some indications as to his state of mind leading up to his death.

"*You know me, Lucy, I'm terrible when I wake up, takes me ages to get me head in the game and my arse in gear. So, right, this evening, alarm went off as usual, 5pm an' I stumble about in the dark trying to gather me wits. I heard the Shatalovas, both of them, arrive from a day out. Think they were drunk cos they were tittering and crashing about and I heard one of them singing 'Happy Birthday' but like, really quietly, like they didn't want to wake me. They're really sweet I think. Anyhoo, I get myself dressed, pack a quick sandwich and I'm out the door. Dog makes a big fuss – bigger than usual for some reason, and halfway down the street I realise what he was trying to tell me. I WAS ONLY NOT WEARING ANY TROUSERS!! What am I like? I was SO embarrassed!*

<u>NOTE:</u> Mrs Watson at 32 Torrance Rd confirmed the above incident, and the timing of the arrival of the Shatalovas. She also claims to have seen the light of 31a go on BEFORE Joe Nowak returned to his room to find his missing trousers. This seems unlikely and we feel it is probably either a misremembering or pot-stirring by Mrs Watson. (See below)

....so I rushed back, went straight into my room, and right, Sis, this is where it got really weird. First off, I had left my light on – I never do that – and I grabbed my trousers, put them on and dashed out, remembering to turn the light out. Honestly I was in such a fog, what with just having woken up and worried I'd miss the bus. But I got halfway down the street when I realized SOMETHING WAS WRONG! And it weren't my trousers. Why was my light on, and...and...I had this image, hazy I know, but I could've sworn Mrs Shatalova and Rosie were in my room, just, like standing there, staring at me as I grabbed my trousers and dashed out. "I'm going mad", I think to myself, and I can see on the bus shelter that the bus is

delayed so I rush back to the flat. Dog is going bananas. In the front door, down the stairs and BANG! Guess what. IT WAS LOCKED! I don't remember, in my haste, locking my door!! Spooky, right? I'm fumbling in the dark for me keys, sure I can hear something in my flat, so I thinks, best ask Rosie, so I knock on her door, but there's no answer. Must be out. Waited a mo, gave up and went back to my door. I put my key in the lock and it gets stuck, won't turn. I jab it in a few times and suddenly it goes in, I turn it, open the door ....and nothing. Nobody there. Light off. BUT.... but...dunno, a sixth sense or something....jus' didn't feel right. Then I jumped out of my skin as someone tapped me on the shoulder, turned round an' got the shock of me life. Rosie is standing RIGHT BEHIND ME and she's, like, panting, really sweaty, like she's been jogging. She's not the jogging type and anyway she's dressed like Mrs Kronka, the Madam at the brothel in Groszny Lukas took me to...oh...you didn't know about that?...anyhoo...... She assures me everything is ok and she hurries me off to the bus stop. It was a weird start to my shift I have to tell you, left me out of sorts all night.

Additional information from Mrs Watson, while it corroborates Joe Nowak's story, also goes on about the lights and references Mrs and Ms Shatalova, (see Case File No 232456).

Mrs Watson reported that the light went on and off regularly in the flat 31a, even when nobody was home. But on the night in question, she saw Joe Nowak depart around 5.30pm, but not wearing any trousers. He must have realized his mistake because he rushed back, but Mrs Watson swears the light came on BEFORE he returned. Having obviously put on his trousers he exited the flat, got to the bus stop then chose to return to his flat a second time. Mrs Watson now reports that she saw Rosie Shatalova exit through the pavement-level window (*note in pencil "must've been a tight squeeze"*) and then reach in and attempt to pull her mother through the same window. Unfortunately, it seems Ludmilla Shatalova became stuck, so Rosie abandoned her and dashed back into the house, emerging a few moments later with Joe Nowak just as Ludmilla Shatalova slid back into the room. Rosie saw Joe onto the bus, then ran back to the house. The light of 31a stayed on for a while and switched off just as Mr Jones entered the property (Case File No 232457).

MR JONES

"Something is wrong. Very wrong. I'm standing in front of my flat and I'm about to insert my key when... the door...just swings open. Unlocked. Open. All day. I would never leave the door unlocked, not knowing what I know. Knowing what is hidden. Then, toilet flush and suddenly Rosie is standing right behind me. Except she's sweating, an' she's so close I can see her concealer starting on run on her forehead.

"You alright, Rosie? Been joggin' or something?" I ask her. She's panting, struggling for breath.

"Yeah, Mr Jones, that's right. Gotta keep fit, eh!" and she scuttles back to her room. Except I notice she's wearing high heels and skin- tight trousers showing every crack and bump.

I'm standing on the threshold of my room and a thousand thoughts are running through my brain. None of them good. Have the Shatalova's been snooping in my room? Did I catch them at it? Or has…. god forbid…..*she* been here? I scan the room – everything seems to be in order, nothing out of place. Then I see them. Curtains. Closed. I never leave them closed. I always draw them before I leave…. don't I? Didn't I? Now I'm doubting myself. But it doesn't make sense, unless someone came into my room and closed the curtains, if they were doing something they shouldn't, not with the curtain-twitcher opposite. I swear she's retired M15, that woman. But thoughts about the curtains are brushed aside when I notice the smell. There's always an underlying smell here which I can't put my finger on, sometimes it's like a pot noodle smell, sometimes it's a, I dunno, like a rotting smell. Them next door always talk about drains, and smelly neighbours, but sometimes – like now – it seems particularly strong.

First things first. I need to unload. How many times have I done this, briefcase on the table and unlock. Innocuous enough, but a little twist here and the case reveals it's secret. Staring back at me, my past, my present and my future. Bundled neatly in 10's, 20's and 50's is about £20,000 in cash. Holy moly, I continue to get away with it, but it needs stashing.

Check the door is locked, chair into the alcove under the vent, a coin to unscrew the plastic bolt and the vent falls away. There it is. To be precise – I am an accountant after all - £2,350,180. All untraceable though no doubt contaminated with smack, snow, dust, and the rest. Crammed into the air-conditioning duct, with every available space used to its fullest extent, bound in plastic, elastic bands, in brown sheaths, every note with a story to tell, ultimately finding their way to a smackhead's pocket or a rich wastrel's wallet and handed over for a moment of release, escape, excitement and oblivion. From the dusty fields of Afghanistan and the verdant forests of Columbia comes the product, secreted through intricate pathways of deceit that would confound Daedelus and outfox Theseus. In the other direction from the royal mint, finely crafted polymers adorned with the upstanding figures of our illustrious past - Jane Austen, JW Turner, Alan Turing and the godfather of our financial free-for-all, Adam Smith. How many lives do both product and finance pass through till they reach the grasping hands of Lulu Gold and my office safe? How much money does one person need? Research somewhere stated that in excess of £60,000 per annum won't make us any happier. I beg to differ. I've got two mill plus stashed away and I'm happy as Larry. Or I will be when I stop this madness and move on. And I think I've reached peak stash. I cannot for the life of me fit another centime into this damn hole. Nope. Stuffed full to Dolly's Wax as my Gran used to say. And I'm standing there, "*hovering like a fly, waiting for a windshield on the freeway*" when there's a knock at the bloody door.

ROSIE

Back in her flat after the shenanigans of the morning, Rosie caught her breath.

"Christ alive, Mum, I swear to God this is going to be the end of me! Dead on me twenty first of a coronary"

"Ach, girl, get some spunk" said her mother. "So the idiot forgot his trousers, came back in, went out, came back – the thing is, we dealt with it, Ok. No problem"

"Would've gone smoother if you wasn't such a lard-arse, Mum…."

"He he he I thought I would pop like ripe bilberry."

"yeah…ha ha ha, I'd have pulled yer arms out their sockets. Bet ol' Mrs Watson burst a blood vessel trying to work out what was happening".

"But Mr Jones, he suspects nothing, no?"

"Well….."

"Well what?"

"We…er…we didn't get the door locked. As he came into the house you shot off here and I made it to the bog just in time but didn't get to lock up. I flushed the chain an' came out all innocent like, an' he was just standing there, key in his hand, staring at the open door. I made a few pleasantries an' scarpered."

"Ok so. Could be big trouble with the clever man. We need to check in with Mr Jones. You go. Grab rent book; it is due now anyway."

The two women bustled about, getting the book, pen, checking the mirror and were soon standing outside 31a. Rosie knocked.

"What is it?" came a strangely strangled cry from Mr Jones.

"Nothing, dearie, just the rent" said Ludmilla, raising an eyebrow to her daughter.

"One moment…just…I'm…..hang on…"

Both heard a few bumps and bangs, and then the door was unlocked and flew open. A red-faced Mr Jones stood there.

"Well, ain't you the man of mystery, Mr Jones" said Rosie coyly. "Got yer door locked, keepin' a woman in there?"

"No…no not at all. What do you want?"

"Rent please" said Ludmilla brusquely and pushed her way past Rosie into the flat and stopped at the table.

"Where chair please?" said Ludmilla.

On her heels, Mr Jones realized he had left the chair against the wall underneath the vent. He swerved towards it and in that moment, everything changed. Ludmilla Shatalova's desire to park her considerable backside now set in motion 24 hours of Jacobean horror.

As his back was turned, Rosie noticed a sheaf of banknotes sticking out a miniscule amount from the briefcase lid. She swiftly raised the lid and revealed to her mother and herself a jumbled pile of assorted banknotes, some in rolls, some in sheaths and some in plastic bags. Never having seen a large amount of money before they couldn't immediately process how much was there, but as experts of knowing the value of everything, they correctly surmised the pile of £10, £20, and £50 notes added up to…. a lot. Rosie dropped the lid.

The almost imperceptible 'thud' of the lid reached the ears of Mr Jones as his hand spun the chair round. With a brain so used to weighing up risk, options, and opportunities, Mr Jones took less than a nano-second to process what might have just happened, what that meant for him, for the Shatalovas and for his future. He was already planning ahead as he pushed the chair into the back of Ludmilla's legs, causing her to sit abruptly.

"One month please Mr Jones" said Lundmilla, opening the rent book and proffering him a pen. He signed, reached into his pocket, and pulled out a thin wallet. He plucked the notes with his thin, boney fingers, aware that the Shatalovas were watching him like a hawk. He handed over the money and snapped the book shut, forcing Ludmilla to swiftly extract her chubby fingers. For a moment there was silence.

"Right then, you haf a lovely evenink" said Ludmilla as she stood and pushed back the chair. She caught Rosie's eye and raised an eyebrow, then walked out of the room. Rosie turned as if to go then stopped. She lingered.

'She never lingers' thought Mr Jones.

"So, going out tonight. Splashing yer hard-earned cash on a lady friend, maybe up Sheiks?"

"No….no, staying in" said Mr Jones flatly, not knowing what Sheiks was.

"That's a shame. It's my birthday. 21 today, keys to the door and all that. I'm all grown up now, the world is my oyster an' I feel like cutting loose. Sure you don't want to take a young lady out?"

"Quite sure, and thanks for the offer, but I've got some work hanging over me," said Mr Jones, not moving from the table.

"Suit yerself. But the offer's there. Ends at midnight." Rosie turned and walked to the door, unnecessarily slowly. Mr Jones watched her go blankly, but by the time she reached the door he was watching her like a randy, middle-aged bloke who hadn't held a woman for so long. She turned, gave him a little smile, and shut the door.

MR JONES

"That was close. Too close. Did they see anything? Thought I heard the case shut, wouldn't put it passed those two, conniving sods the pair of them.. Well, boyo, I reckon that's made up your mind. You're finished. Time to pack up and go. End of the week, when you've got the tickets booked, you're out of here. Maldives? Australia? Somewhere to lay low, invest, start over. She won't know where to start looking. She can scour the valleys as long as she wants, she won't find anybody even remotely related to me that she can get her claws into. I'm the nowhere man, she'll seek me here, she'll seek me there, but I'll be a ghost, the one that got away. If she wasn't such a psycho she's let it go – a few mill is a drop in her ocean – but that's not how she operates. That's not what made her.

I know what that Rosie is made of, I saw it as she walked out. Walked? That wasn't a walk, that was parade of goods for purchase. All curve and sway. Twenty-one, eh! I remember being twenty-one. Holed up at university sweating over textbooks. Well, I've paid my dues. I've a first -class ticket to the party. But. Gotta empty the case! How many times have I scoured this room for hidey holes? Nothing. Just a loose floorboard with evidence of mice, not putting my retirement fund at the mercy of hungry rodents. And I'm walking around my room like a fool with £20,000 in cash in his arms when there another knock at the door. This time gentler, secret. Nothing for it, just put the dosh back in the case, shut it this time, and open the door.

"Allo handsome" Rosie says, all coy like, draping herself against the doorframe. A Rita Hayworth in modern dress. She looks like she's been poured into it, she's like a rump steak to a starving man. She looks magnificent.

She looks trouble.

I know her type and I know mine. I've been here before, I know where this can lead, I've been there, got me into a lot of trouble, see. I'm a soft touch for the feminine wiles, call it my passionate Welsh heart if you like, but I've no intention of sliding back into the chaos of my previous life.

"What?" I ask as curtly as I could.

"I'm dressed like bleedin' Cleopatra and he asks 'what?' You fer real?"

"it's just that…"

"D'ya like it? Shall I twirl?" She twirled. I may have the body of Jack Spratt, but I like a woman with curves, and she has them in spades.

"It's very…. nice…. suits you," I manage to stammer. Christ I'm a weak sod.

"Nice? Well, it's a start. It's an outfit that needs to be seen in, doncha think. Mum's gone to bed early and here's me, dressed to the nines on me twenty first and looking for some fun! How about you and me hit the town, a few bars, maybe a dance at Sheiks, then see how the rest of the night pans out, if you get me drift".

I got her drift. Suddenly the whole night swam before my eyes, the drinks, the laughs, the fumbled caresses and sweaty kisses. And I'm looking at her and I'm hard. I'm faint there's so much blood in my prick. I'm staring at her, her tasselled chassis, all cleavage, big blue eyes and full red lips. Blow it, why not! I'm as rich as a footballer, Championship not Premiership, but I've plenty, so why not let my hair down. I've earned it, and I'm going to have to get use to the party lifestyle. What better place to start than Bognor with a willing 21 year old..

I play it cool.

"Ok. Why not. I need a break. I'll just fetch me jacket."

I make sure the briefcase is shut and put it on the floor beside the table. Jacket on, wallet in pocket, I lock the door behind me. Rosie takes my arm. With her heels she towers over me.

"Well, this is a turn up fer the books, you an' me all this time, jus' over the corridor from each other. An' now look at us! So Mike – can I call you Mike? - where first?" She twitters on as we climb the steps and walk out into the salty air of "a Bognor late autumn evening."

LUDMILLA

Ludmilla heard the door slam and knew her clever daughter had successfully snared Mr Jones for the evening, giving her plenty of time. To make sure, she went to the front door and gingerly stuck her head out. Rosie and Mr Jones were making their way down the road – she could hear Rosie screeching in the still night air. She glanced around and scurried back inside. She failed to notice the black Mercedes parked 50 feet down on the opposite side of the road.

She unlocked 31a and did a pantomime tiptoe across to the table, although she knew nobody was in the flat. A quick glance around and she spotted the briefcase on the floor. Placing it silently on the table she flipped open the clasps, thankful it hadn't been locked, and opened the lid. Money was crammed into the case, though it was immediately evident to her that a considerable pile was missing. That meant that – either he took thousands out with him (unlikely) – or that somewhere in the flat he had a private stash. She started to mutter in Ukrainian and blurted out the occasional giggle. This was better than anything she had ever envisioned for herself. Or her daughter. This thin streak of piss of a man was her golden ticket. Life was about to get much, much better for the Shatalovas.

She knew she'd have to wait to do a thorough search when Rosie was back, but for now, she took out a bundle of £20 notes, slid out a sizeable number from the middle, returned what was left and shut the case. Congratulating herself she repeated the tiptoe across the floor, exited 31a and locked the door behind her.

LULU GOLD

With its discrete darkened glass and small diesel heater, the Mercedes Benz Series 3 was perfect as a stake-out vehicle. Lulu Gold sat, impassive, in the passenger seat while Milo relaxed beside her. In the back, slouched and bored lay Nosmo. There had been some small talk at first, but both men knew when to shut up and wait for Miss Gold to lead the talk. They had watched Mr Jones depart with an over-dressed young woman that Milo presumed was a prostitute, but Nosmo said he didn't recognize her. Gold said nothing so the car settled down into watch and wait mode. To be honest, Gold had suggested the outing just to see the lay of the land after she had the results back from a Mayfair company of investigative accountants. They had spent several weeks poring over her books and had identified some glaring errors that couldn't be mere oversights. Mr Jones's number was up!

Gold shifted her position.

"Where are we with the Itchenor property?" she asked. "Did the boys do a good job getting it ready for the refurb?"

"Yeah, all sorted" said Milo. "They did a right proper number on it, apparently. Smashed in walls, removed all the plumbing, ripped out the electrics. Got it ready for the refurb so when the family got in there, poor sods, they didn't have much choice. You remember The Skankers, early eighties? It's that family. They were looking to inherit a tidy sum, the son's a drama student or something, needs to pay off his student loan. All they got was a building site. Still, they'll see sense. The Agents made an offer on our behalf. They'll take the offer, so we're ready to move on the application – should only take a couple of months."

"No complications?"

"Well, the agent started making noises about wanting a bigger cut, so I showed her the knife and asked where she wanted the cut. She's happy now."

Lulu Gold exhaled and nodded. Milo knew this was her way of showing approval.

"I think we've spent enough time sitting here. I suggest we use his absence for the evening to affect an entry and a swift search of his premises." Lulu pulled on some leather gloves. "No noise, boys, don't want that Russian hippopotamus storming in on us.

Out in the chill November air, they pulled their expensive camel hair coats up to their necks and raised the collars. Gold led the way, across the street, the two men a respectful distance behind, eyes darting left and right. The road was deserted. They stopped outside the property.

"Any suggestions?" asked Gold

"Might be a bit tricky forcing the lock inside" said Nosmo. "The Russian could come out an any time. We need to open the door from the inside, then when it's done, you come straight in off the street. Let me try the window."

He knelt, took out a flat piece of metal and inserted it around the lock. A few seconds later the window shifted and opened.

"I'll pop in and check the lock. Won't take a mo."

Nosmo slid his wiry, muscled frame through the window and touched down on the bed beneath. A few moments later he popped his head back up.

"It's an old lock, easily picked. I'll open inside and let you in."

Gold and Milo moved away from the window and opened the door to the basement flats. Milo used a small but powerful torch to illuminate the steps down, just as Nosmo opened the door of 31a and let them in, shutting the door silently behind them. They stood, not breathing, eyes getting use to the dark.

"What the fuck is that smell?" asked Nosmo, crinkling his nose distastefully.

"That, Nosmo, is the reek of poverty, mingling with odours of loneliness, sexual frustration and, I suspect, thievery".

"Very poetic, Ma'am" said Milo. "I can only smell Pot Noodle".

The three of them simultaneously suppressed a laugh.

"Right then, to work. Minimal torches boys. Don't want nosey neighbours seeing flashes from inside. Don't disturb anything. I don't want him to suspect."

The three of them spread out across the small bedsit. Milo got to the table, the briefcase sitting on it where Ludmilla had left it. He clicked open the clasps, drawing a 'tsk' of disapproval from Gold as the 'thunk-thunk' reverberated around the empty flat. He opened the case.

"Well, that was easy. Ma'am?" He stood back as Gold and Nosmo stepped in to see the bundles of bank notes tumbling out of the case.

"Got the bastard" muttered Nosmo.

"Mmmmm. Very good. But small change." Gold then pulled from her pocket a small electronic device, no bigger than a book of matches. She slid it into one of the pockets of the case."

"There. We'll know his movements if this case is with him. Keep looking. I'll check the kitchen, Milo, go through his drawers, Nosmo, check under the bed. How stupid can he be?"

The three of them split up. The sodium light of the streetlamps cast long shadows as they moved silently about the room. Nosmo bent down and flipped up the duvet hanging over the bed. Shining a torch underneath he caught sight of a glass box, some sort of aquarium, with a lid. He reached in and pulled it out. It seemed to be empty, just some dried leaves. He took the lid off, discarding an old glove he found on top, and put it to one side, then reached in and felt amongst the debris at the bottom of the box.

Nosmo, used to inflicting pain on others from a position of power and cruel authority, was surprised to feel a sharp, intense jab to the back of his hand. Snatching back his arm, he stood up and rubbed the hand hard, cursing under his breath. He looked about him. Lulu Gold was in the kitchen and Milo had his head down in a chest of drawers.

"Sod it." He muttered under his breath.

He bent and tried to put the lid back on, but it wouldn't fit easily, so he pushed the glass box back under the bed with his foot. He looked about him to see if the others were close by and was perturbed to realise his head was swimming. His vision momentarily blurred, then popped back into focus, then blurred again. Trying to quell a rising sense of panic, he stepped away from the bed, but each step was like a sledgehammer in his brain. He had a blinding headache. He tried to sit down on the bed, missed, and crashed to the floor. Lulu Gold shot out from the kitchen hissing between clenched teeth like a rattled mongoose just as Milo came around the side of the bed. They looked down at the prone form of Nosmo.

"Nosmo, what the actual?" whispered Gold tersely, nudging him with her foot.

Nosmo raised his head and apologised.

"Something bit me. Under the bed. Snake I think."

Milo shone his torch down on his fellow henchman and abruptly stepped back in shock. Gold froze. Nosmo was white as a sheet, his hands clenched into boney claws held tight to his chest.

Suddenly a shaft of light shone under the door. Milo and Gold froze. A door swung shut. Milo pulled out a pistol and reached into his pocket for a silencer. He stepped over to the door as he screwed the silencer on, listening intently at the door. He heard another door open and close, then silence.

"Think someone's in the bog. Must be the mum" whispered Milo. Gold put a hand up, demanding restraint. The two stood stock still in the dark, while at their feet Nosmo writhed and jerked in pain. There was a toilet flush, a door opened, closed, heavy footsteps disappeared down the corridor, then another door opened...and closed. Gold and Milo exhaled. Milo sheathed his gun as Lulu Gold glanced down at her rapidly expiring trusty lieutenant

"Get him out. Now," commanded Gold. Milo pulled Nosmo up by one arm and slung him over his shoulder. Gold opened the door for him. Milo stepped out into the corridor, checked all was clear. Gold went ahead and gave him the nod from the top of the stairs. They shot silently across the road. The Merc unlocked with a 'clunk' and an orange flash, as Gold opened the back door. Milo lay Nosmo across the back seat as Gold fired the engine up, and in seconds they were heading away from Torrance Road.

"Where we taking him, Boss? St Richards?"

"Not risking that. Too many questions. Snake. He said snake. What did he mean by that? Has that bastard got a deadly snake in there, protecting his stash?"

Milo was leaning over the seat, tending to Nosmo. He turned back round.

"He's looking rough."

As the car sped on, through foggy patches rising from the Sussex lowlands, Lulu Gold found herself experiencing feelings. Uncomfortable, unfamiliar feelings. She felt a strange hollowness in her chest. She liked Nosmo, but she wasn't sure there was anything she could do for him.

"We'll take him home, let him sweat it out there. Our Mr Jones. When he comes in tomorrow…". She left the thought hanging but Milo knew exactly what she meant.

PART THREE

'In the midst of chaos, there is
also opportunity'

Sun Tzu

NOVEMBER 3,
EARLY MORNING

MR JONES

"Something is wrong. Very wrong. Holy crap, there's someone in my….. no! NO!! Think, lad, think! Got to break through this fug, man, work out what's going on. Ok, ok, it's coming clearer. Last night. Drinks, food, more drinks, dancing was involved, then shots. Taxi back, God knows what time, then….

And she's still here. What's the time? Strewth, man! Gotta get going. Can't be late for work. Lift back the covers. I'm naked. She's naked. Her face is a mess, make-up everywhere, but man, those curves. Don't even think about it, boy. Get a move on.

"Morning Rosie, I've got to get going, can't be late….Rosie?"

"Mmm? Wha…. What time is it?"

"Er…. just gone 8."

"Jus' gone…what?!"

She throws back the covers, grabs a few bits of clothes from the floor and she's out the door. I can hear her and her mad mother whispering intently outside. Probably getting a low-down on last night. Let them gossip. I've had my fun and I'm moving on. Mind you. Not feeling great if I'm honest. Head's thick for sure but my guts are feeling none too secure. No time for shower, breakfast, just dress and out.

Right, clothes on but my head is spinning. Fresh air will help. Briefcase.... briefcase? Where's the .... what's it doing on the table? I left it.... sure, I left it.... on the floor. I'm getting spooked, I can tell you. Money is all there I think, no time to count. Got to get rid of it now. But where? Can't leave it on the bed, someone might see from outside. Damn it, I'll have to chuck it under the bed. Just reach in and.... hello! What the hell is under my bed? Now to be honest I've never looked under my bed, no need to really, never going to stash 2 mill under the bed, I mean, how stupid do you think I am? But needs must, so here I am, on my knees, and there's a sodding vivarium under the bed, left by a previous tenant no doubt. Covered in dust, loads of dead leaves, but it'll do. Chuck in the money, shove it back under and get off to work.

Oh oh! Stood up to fast.......

ROSIE

Standing in the hall with clothes clasped to preserve her laughable modesty, Rosie was confronted by her mother.

"Mum, why'd'ja let me sleep in, it's gone frickin' 8. We'll never get him out and turned around in time."

"You should think of this before, stupid girl. I'm pacing here, gently knocking, wondering what is going on, I swear, I'm hafing palpitations."

"Let me get dressed and you might have to keep watch. Move it!"

Rosie dashed into her flat, threw on her clothes and dashed out again. The door to 31a was open and she could hear retching sounds from the toilet.

"You alright, Mikey?" she asked

The door flew open, and the two lovers confronted each other for the first time in daylight.

"You've got a bit of…." Rosie pointed to Mike Jones' lapel. He glanced down, spun around and shut the door. Rosie cursed as she listened to an encore of retching. Ludmilla appeared behind her, pulling the cart of belongings.

"He's gone, yes?"

"Christ, no Mum, back off!"

Ludmilla reversed adroitly back into her flat.

"You alright, Mikey" shouted Rosie, trying to hurry him along. Ludmilla appeared beside her.

"You go. Scram, I get him out double quick. You get camera ready." Rosie huffed and disappeared into her flat.

Just then, the front door opened, and Ludmilla froze, as she saw Joe Nowak, bending down and petting the dog. Ludmilla yelped, dashed into her flat and returned immediately with Rosie, who was looking equally appalled, with Ludmilla hissing in her ear. Suddenly the toilet flushed, as Joe came down the stairs. As he tried to turn into his flat, Rosie waylaid him with an arm around his shoulder, leading him towards 31b.

"Well hello, Joe, how's your night been? Looks like you might need a massage…"

"Oh, it was OK thank you, I just need to hit the sack."

"What an excellent idea" said Rosie as she unceremoniously railroaded poor Joe into her flat. Ludmilla watched them disappear and thus missed the sight of Charlie bouncing down the stairs, just as the toilet door opened and Mr Jones emerged looking somewhat greener about the gills.

"Morning sir, you're usually gone by now, don't get to see you" said the young man.

"Mmm, running a bit late, a heavy night…."

"Yeah, well, I saw you last night down Sheiks, who's the lucky boy, eh! Now, are you Jones or Nowak?"

Mr Jones looked confused. "I'm Jones. Mike Jones, 31a, yeah?"

Charlie was suddenly a bit flustered, as he had two lots of post in his hand.

"Yeah…yeah, of course, sorry…er…"

Ludmilla threw herself between the two men, grabbing the post.

"Morning Mr Jones. You the naughty boy by all accounts, underneath that Mr accountant costume, yes? Here's yer post, now shouldn't you be getting off?"

Ludmilla turned him towards the stairs, but he resisted.

"Yes, I need to hurry, but I need my briefcase," and he turned into his room. Charlie was now craning his neck to see if he could catch sight of Rosie through the partially open door of 31b, but Ludmilla intervened.

"Alright Casanova you, hop it, scram, nothing fer you here. Rosie's spoken for."

"Spoken for?" laughed Charlie. "What is this, a Jane Austen novel".

"Ach, clear off you clever bugger", said Ludmilla, giving him a hefty shove towards the door. She dashed back into her own flat. Charlie nearly collided with Mr Jones, exiting his flat. After a brief clown routine of to-me-to-you, the pair extricated themselves from each other. Charlie disappeared up the stairs and Mr Jones, finding that the sudden unexpected spinning motion caused by bumping into Charlie had aggravated his gag reflex, sped into the toilet and slammed the door.

LUDMILLA

Ludmilla had intended to hide briefly in her hallway until the coast was clear, but she inadvertently caught sight of Joe Nowak in Rosie's bedroom, through the door left slightly ajar. Joe was spread-eagled on Rosie's bed and was handcuffed to the headboard. Rosie was on top of him, writhing around and Ludmilla could hear Joe whimpering like an unhappy dog. She had seen enough, Joe would be occupied for a while longer, so she needed to move. Hearing a door slam she peeked out into the corridor and saw Charlie disappearing up the stairs. Mr Jones must be ahead of him.

Ludmilla grabbed the cart and hauled it out into the corridor to 31a. Mr Jones' flat wasn't locked, which would normally have sounded alarm bells for Ludmilla, but this was an emergency, so she ploughed on regardless. She scurried around the flat like a flabby pinball, bouncing between the furniture and the cart, totally engrossed in the task. So engrossed she failed to hear Mr Jones exit from the toilet, pull his door shut and lock it. She missed the brief interaction of Mr Jones and a very strange man momentarily emerging from 31b, de-trousered and manacled, babbling in an incomprehensible language, before being dragged back,

clearly against his will, into 31b. She didn't hear Mr
Jones slam the front door nor the snarling of the dog,
the snapping of his jaws around the Thin Man's ankle.
She completely missed Mr Jones bending down to rub
his painful leg and coming within a gnat's whisker
of eyeballing his landlady through the street-level
window as she stripped his room of all his possessions
and replaced them with those of the unfortunate Joe
Nowak. Unbelievably, she avoided being caught mid-
change, but as she finished, she careened into the
locked door. Her considerable nose now bleeding and
her wig askew, she fumbled with her keys and unlocked
the errant door and stepped out into the corridor, just
as Joe fell out – actually fell out - of 31b. He managed
to face plant into the sad, threadbare carpet, allowing
Ludmilla time to change tack and swerve into the
toilet, trolley in tow.

    She sat down on the toilet and thought through her
options. Big ones. Was it time to stop this crazy life?
Unbeknownst to Rosie, Ludmilla had been squirreling
away money this last year, knowing that she needed
a get-out, an insurance policy if things ever got out
of hand. For a woman used to living on her wits,
planning for the worst and living for the now, she was
acutely aware that her rent charade could tumble at
any moment. She knew that what she was doing was
not technically illegal, so she wouldn't have to flee the

country, wouldn't spend time in prison or do the things she had had to do to get herself out of trouble in the past. And anyway, this was Britain, not Soviet Russia nor independent Ukraine where the police had only a passing knowledge of the law and where a position of authority was all that was needed to whisk people off the street or close down a house. She liked it here. She liked these funny people, where humour was a weapon and a mask, where people kept their space like starlings on a telegraph wire and were permanently in thrall to a better yesterday. Ludmilla felt her Soviet soul was somehow at home in Bognor Regis. Sure, they had gangsters here, just like home, but at least here there was a chance that they might get caught.

Ludmilla stood and flushed the chain for the sake of appearances. She had heard Joe's door shut so she knew he was safely ensconced in his room, the funny man. She opened the door, peeked out, saw the coast was clear so scuttled down the corridor into her flat, trolley in tow. She was greeted by Rosie, red-faced and in a state of dishabille, with a look of unquenchable fury in her eyes.

SLOW JOE

WEST SUSSEX POLICE, BOGNOR DIVISION:
INVESTIGATION INTO THE UNEXPLAINED
DEATH OF JOE NOWAK.

On the 3rd of November at some point in the morning, Lucy Nowak received what would be the last call from her brother Joe. She recounted to PC Ricketts the following;

"Joe had rung me on the morning of the 3rd, which was unusual because normally he was asleep by then after his night shift. He was babbling quite a lot and I could tell he was really stressed and unhappy, and it took me quite a while to get him to calm down and tell me clearly what the problem was.

It seems the morning had started badly. He arrived back to his flat about 8.15 am as usual, played briefly with the dog outside, but then met Rosie in the corridor. He described her as behaving 'with a weird aggression towards me', frog-marched him into her flat and…. well, officer, I know this is going to sound far-fetched, and I know our Joe is a bit simple, but basically, it sounds like she … assaulted…him. She tied him to the bed! She stripped him virtually naked, poor Joe. She was doing things he had only heard about and was very free with exposing parts of her body to Joe he had only – well – dreamt about. But he also said she was acting very strangely, running in and out of the bedroom, coming back and inflicting more torture on him, y'know, flicking her hair on his chest and doing things…. with her mouth. He finally managed to escape. He must've been so upset – I think possibly he was still a virgin, despite being married to that terrible woman, I can't see her allowing anybody near her that didn't look *like Brad Pitt. He was clearly out of sorts, and said he tried to calm himself down by going into his usual routine, you know, catching a mouse and feeding it to his snake whilst listening to Indian pipe music. But today, he pulled out his snake thingy, what's the word in English? No!! Not that, no you idiot, not HIS....no, where he kept the snake. Vivarium? Oh, ok, yes, well, that. And guess what! The lid was loose, and the snake gone, and in its place, a stash of cash. Joe, bless him, had no idea what was going on, he's a very honest boy and he'd be very worried that the money wasn't his. Then he thought that maybe someone had come and taken the snake and had left the money by way of compensation. I wouldn't put it past some of his work mates, they sound like not a very nice bunch of men. In this respect your country is very like Poland.*

So now Joe, he is in a pickle. He thinks the snake is loose somewhere in the flat or has been taken and replaced by a considerable amount of money.

Note: The transcript takes a break here, but Det Supt Bovey has added a note that PC Ricketts was censored by HR for making unhelpful and unsolicited approaches to Lucy Nowak, with whom Ricketts seems to have formed a loose relationship and was seeking to encourage her to visit Bognor, sooner rather than later so he could 'take her down Sheiks'. Det Supt Bovey did later interview Ms Nowak where she made some serious and enlightening allegations that has further shed light on how the 3rd ^{of} November proceeded, leading ultimately to the death of Joe Nowak.

WHAT THE DOG SAW.

With his canine sense of smell, Dog knew that the Thin Man was not well. The smell intrigued him, it was both edible and repulsive. Dog bit and then let go.

The Nice Man had arrived, but the usual routine, which the dog watched with keen interest, knowing that at some point he would be invited into through the window and on to the man's deliciously odiferous bed, this routine was unexpectedly abandoned. Instead, the man put on his strange sounds from the metal box, sounds that brought forth even stranger whimpers from the Dog, from behind the grimey glass window. He watched the familiar feeding of the snake, the appearance of which terrified Dog and made his hair stand on end, but this morning, no snake appeared, and the man's mood seemed to change significantly. He had found lots of paper in different colours – Dog recognised this paper as highly prized, since his old master often sat with large piles of it on his kitchen table, just staring at it – but the Nice Man seemed suddenly very nervous and put the coloured paper back.

Dog watched his friend with canine concern. The Nice Man stood stock still, holding a dead mouse in his hand by the tail. Dog could sense the raised heartbeat, the quickening of the breath. The Nice Man was .... listening. Watching, nervously, eyes flicking around the room. With his ability to empathise with human emotions and intentions, Dog realised, with rising dread, that the snake had escaped and that the Nice Man was very, very scared. Slowly the man turned around, his eyes scanning the room. He tiptoed carefully across the room and laid the mouse on the edge of the table. He wafted his hands over it, and even through the glass, Dog picked up the smell of dead mouse. Dog growled his approval at the Nice Man's hunting technique. Any admiration was short-lived, as he saw the man then walk around the room, clicking his fingers and making a kissing sound with his lips. Dog had seen this behaviour many times before, when strangers approached him in the street, to pat or stroke him, and sometimes to try and grab him. He understood the thinking behind the beckoning gesture but knew instinctively it was wasted on a snake. Nice Man quickly realised this too and stopped. He reached over to the metal box and pressed it, making the high-pitched noise that caused the Dog to whimper to finally stop. Dog knew the snake seemed to like this noise – or at least so the man thought – it was probably more to do with the association of noise and mouse.

If the snake had indeed escaped and was now roaming under floorboards, inside cupboards and slithering between the walls, no amount of coaxing was going to help. Dog knew that the snake would rather be free and feasting on live mouse. He'd seen the mice out at play during the day when the man slept. They were many, and never seemed to dwindle despite the voracious appetite of the somnambulant reptile.

However clever the Dog was, he couldn't see into the soul of Joe Nowak. Dog thought Joe was concerned about losing his snake. Joe, however, was utterly paralysed by the thought of other people suffering at the fangs of Pat – that he might be responsible for the death or injury to anyone in the flat, Rosie or Ludmilla. And then, as adrenalin coursed around his body at these gruesome thoughts, his sympathetic nervous system went into overdrive when he realised that Ludmilla might discover he was breaking the cardinal rule of the flat – NO PETS ALLOWED.

Dog watched, utterly engrossed, ears pricked, nose twitching as he watched the Nice Man pick up the glass box and start to move around the room, searching for the snake. He seemed to cover every inch, under things, inside drawers, under the cupboard, around the bed....so engrossed was Dog, so concerned for the Man's welfare, Dog completely missed the return of the Thin Man. He caught the smell too late to bark out a warning to the Nice Man. He looked on, helpless as the Nice Man disappeared into the room where the food came from just as the Thin Man walked down the steps.

MR JONES

"Stupid, stupid idiot. What was I thinking? Said she was trouble and now look what's happened. My head is spinning, man. Can't believe I've got anything left in the stomach except bile. Got halfway to work and realised I wasn't going to make it, had to step off and heave onto the verge. Not the dignified behaviour of a man with 2 mill to his name. So, I called up Milo on the mobile and said I was sick as a dog and would have to take the day off, and he was well rude, hardly said a word, no 'Oh dear Mr Jones, hope you feel better soon' and the like. Just grunted at me and put the phone down.

So here I am, home again. The mangy mutt for some reason doesn't attack me, which is a bonus on a bad day, but I can feel the gorge rising and make it to the bog just in time. Dry heaving must be God's clearest way of showing his displeasure at one's behaviour, I reckon. Squeezing out thimbles of bile after such huge abdominal constrictions is the purest example of futility. And weirdly, I'm on the big white phone to Jesus when I can hear Indian restaurant music playing somewhere. Must be next door, coming through the pipes or something, though they're not Indian, they're Bulgarian. Terrible whiney noise like a snake charmer pipe thingy. Suddenly it stops. Like I said. Weird.

I've got some serious thinking to do. Maybe this day at home is what I've been waiting for. I'll have a lie-down, recover my spirits and then pack 'n' dash. Make some calls later, but first things first, I need to disappear. Tonight, under the cover of darkness, I shall finally be shot of sodding Bognor Regis.

My head is pounding to, just hurts to open my eyes. Into my room, drop the case, flop onto the bed. Sleep.

SLOW JOE

WEST SUSSEX POLICE, BOGNOR DIVISION: INVESTIGATION INTO THE UNEXPLAINED DEATH OF JOE NOWAK; (Det Supt Bovey is leading this investigation and has removed PC Ricketts from duties associated with this case. Det Supt Bovey continued the interviews with Lucy Nowak himself, and this picks up where the previous interview was suspended.)

'I'd like to take this opportunity to apologise, Ms Nowak, for the behavior of Constable Ricketts. Sad to report his marriage has broken up recently and he's been under a lot of strain...."

"I understand, Detective Bovey, being propositioned by a policeman is not unusual in Poland, and I expected better things of the great British Bobby"

"Your English is excellent, Ms Nowak. Where did you learn it?"

"Please, my name is Lucy, and I learn English at school. For all the problems with the old regime in Poland, education was a high priority, and I am lucky to be old enough to benefit. Now of course these skurwysyn politicians are making it difficult for women, you see. Maybe I should come to England….."

"Well…. I'm sure you'd be very welcome…. but before I get sidetracked…. could you pick up from before? The phone-call with Joe later that day. He told you he realized his snake was missing so went looking for it."

"Precisely, this is what I am telling Mr Ricketts. Joe is terrified the snake is going to jump out at him, so he has the vivarium, still with this money in it, and he's going around the flat looking for the snake. He tries the dead mouse, nothing, so he leaves the mouse on the table, right, then he goes into the kitchen and carefully looks through all the cupboards, making sure he doesn't make any sudden noises. No joy there so he tiptoes back into the bedroom, he says he tried the Indian music again and then, oh my God, can you imagine…he sees…. the door is open a bit! Joe didn't know snakes could open doors….! Well, obviously, they can't, and we know now what was going on but at the

time…it chilled poor Joe to the core he said. So, he hurried
out of the room, had a look around and saw the toilet door
ajar so he goes in and has a good search in there…..

MR JONES

"…..what in God's name is that racket? Indian music?
In my room? What the blazes is going on? There's
nothing worse than being roused from deep slumber,
I can tell you, not with my head as it is. How the hell
did the radio turn itself on…oh, it's a cassette. Why is
there a cassette of…let's see…'The Sounds of India'….
in my radio? Never been there before, I wouldn't put it
past those damn Shatalovas to play tricks on me. Evil
cows. Christ my head is spinning, sit quick, lad, before
you keel over.

I sit at the table and there, right in front of me,
laid out like a votive offering to some pagan God, is a
dead mouse. A dead mouse with a tiny drop of blood
congealed on its nose. Can this day get any worse? I've
had it with this place. Those scheming cows have some
answering to do.

Mouse in hand…well, hanging by a tail…I march
to their flat and bang loudly on their door, regretting
the skull-crunching noise immediately.

ROSIE

Rosie was in the middle of a major set-to with her mother over the events of the morning, after a night where she basically prostituted herself so her mother could scope out 31a.

"Why'da find then, while I was selling my soul, huh?"

"What I find, ungrateful daughter, is money. Briefcase stashed with money."

"What'd'ya nick and where's my share?"

"I took nothing! Too obvious it was us. No, we must be clever about this, we must play Mr Jones like a fish, yes? I think there is more money, somewhere in that flat. Mr Jones the accountant has been getting creative, no? So now we play him. You, clever girl haf got him hooked, now we must reel him in. Carefully cos he could slip the hook any time, Ok? Slowly does it, no rush, he does not suspect, not until we find what he is hiding."

"And how do we do this, with old Slow Joe in there when Mikey ain't?"

Just then there was a hammering at the door. Rosie swore and stomped off to the front door expecting to be confronted by an indignant Joe about his treatment earlier that morning. She flung open the door but before she could speak a mouse, hanging by its tail, was thrust into her face. She reared back to take in the grizzly beast, refocused, and saw a red-faced Mike Jones staring at her.

"What the hell is the meaning of this, Rosie? A dead mouse…really? On my table? What is this, a threat? Some weird post-coital gift from Ukrainian folklore, huh?"

"Mikey…I…what…. I don't understand?"

"There's a dead mouse…on my table. It looks like it's had its brains dashed out. Explain.."

"My goodness, I've no idea. Maybe it just died there."

"Maybe it just….? They're cunning bastards, granted, and acrobatic, but to scale up onto the table and…. well, then what?" Assaulted by a baseball bat-wielding rival gang of Bognor rodents? Overwhelmed by the futility of life it bashes its own brains out on the table?"

"No need to get…. what the…I mean…YOU'RE HOME!"

"Course I'm fecking home, I'm not a hologram sent from the office. Your idea of a good night has right buggered my day, I can tell you that, there'll be no repeat of last night's shenanigans."

"But…but…why're you home…you should be at work?"

"I know I should, but I've been chucking my guts up all morning, no thanks to you. So, what are you going to do about the vermin infestation?"

"Your room….." Rosie stammered but couldn't form the words to ask if there was another man in the room with him. In the charged silence of the moment, Mike Jones grabbed Rosie's wrist and marched her out of the flat and into his. Rosie tried to pull away, but he was insistent. She froze as she entered the room. Where was Joe Nowak?

LUCY'S TESTIMONY (cont.d)

…. but he has no joy in the bathroom, so he heads back into his room. Poor Joe, he's so stressed out, and don't forget he's come off the back of a long night shift, so he puts the vivarium down, he said, as it was so heavy, onto the table, and that's when he saw it."

"Saw what, Miss…. Lucy? What did he see?"

"More a question of what he didn't see. He didn't see a mouse. It was gone. So the snake was around somewhere in the room. Or the kitchen. Joe said he nearly wet himself when he realized the snake was so close. He thought it must be in the kitchen, so he emptied all the money out onto the table – it was making it too heavy – and went back into the kitchen, just as that band went past outside."

"Band? I've got no record of a band?"

'Oh yes, Joe was a big fan. Lots of young girls with sticks, you know, like the Americans. Marching. He sees them in the park in Bognor, performing.

"Ah! The Southern Belles! My daughter is one of them. They're a majorettes marching troupe. I remember, they had time off school to rehearse for the big November the 5th street party."

"You have a party in the middle of November? What is the celebration?"

"It's Guy Fawkes. It's a historical ...thing. Celebrating a.... well...we're burning the traitors who tried to blow up the houses of Parliament. Catholics."

"You're.... burning.... Catholics?"

"Well, just effigies, you know, dummies. Not real Catholics. Not any more.... (there is a very long pause here in the tape) .... Lucy? You still there?"

"I'm here."

"You were saying...the band? Joe in the kitchen?"

"Yes. Joe heard the band approaching just as he went into the kitchen, so he shut the door to keep the noise out. Didn't want to scare the snake. Apparently he says the band is not too good. The clarinet is very high and screechy."

"Ah. My daughter is their clarinetist"

MR JONES

"I march straight in, dragging Rosie with me, her mother just a few steps behind, and the offending dead mouse in my hand. Outside, in a juxtaposition it is hard to fathom, a God-awful racket struck up – I think it was the 'Stars and Stripes' but frankly it was so bad it could've been 'Zombie' by Radiohead. I'm really bristling now with righteous indignation by the way I'm being treated by these two harridans, so I stop and point triumphantly at the exact spot where the mouse met its maker. And there, just…. sitting there… on the table….my latest stash of cash. Thousands of pounds, bundled, rolled, folded, strewn out on the table. Another offering? A bribe? A warning? My brain froze right there and then, I just couldn't explain the circumstances that would lead to this. Then the mother spoke.

"Nice wad, Mr Jones." I swear she was trying to be sexy. I glanced back at the conniving pair, and I could see their plucked, threaded, sculpted, laminated, waxed, painted, and tinted sodding eyebrows raising in a signal I recognized all too well. They were on to me. I was speechless. This wasn't happening. Not now. Not to me, Mike meticulously planned and deftly executed Jones! This was an A1 disaster.

I push the two of them out of the room and slam the door. I needed to think and think fast. First things first – stash the cash. Nothing for it. I was going to have to try and cram it into the vent. I scoop the lot up into my arms as the marching band filed past the window.

I glance out – all I could see were white leatherette boots definitely not marching in time, and the frigging dog being driven wild by the screeching of the terrible clarinetist. I grab the chair, stuck it against the wall and prised off the vent and started to try and stuff the rolls of notes in. I had bloody Genesis pinging into my brain, my number one album of all time, 'The Lamb Lies Down on Broadway.' *'There's Howard Hughes in Blue Suede shoes, watching all the Majorettes smoking Winston Cigarettes. And as the song and dance begins, the children play at home, with needles. Needles and pins.'* I'm singing under my breath, manically stuffing cash into the hole, but it won't all fit. I refit the vent and step down. Where oh where can I store this cash???

LUDMILLA and ROSIE

Her brain working overtime, the arch schemer was already processing options as she and Rosie were unceremoniously tumbled out of into the corridor. Ludmilla knew exactly what to do. With Rosie veering between whimpering pathetically and shouting in rage, Ludmilla calmly strode into her kitchen, opened the cupboard under the sink and gingerly eased her considerable frame down onto her knees. She peered deep into the recesses of the cupboard, an assemblage of bottles, containers, rags, and tools that had served their purpose once and now stood, gathering dust and grime from slowly dripping wastepipes. She spied what she was looking for. Amongst the snazzy packaging of carpet cleaners, upholstery foam and silver polish, she saw a plain brown bottle with a faded label. Like Indiana Jones spying the Holy Grail, she recognized its simplicity, and its deadly contents. She reached in and carefully pulled it out.

"There we go. This will sort it out."

"What's that. Mother's ruin?"

Ludmilla ignored – or didn't understand her daughters sarcastic remark but held the bottle in front of her.

"This is a present from your Uncle Vlad"

"Is that a skull and crossbones on the label"

"This is special concoction. Vlad was a scientist… a chemist… for the KGB. He made things that you don't mess with. He gave me this bottle as a parting gift when I leave for England. Pretended it was Vodka. Just glad customs didn't ask me to take swig, see? This is most deadly poison in Ukraine. For vermin, dogs, cats, tiny dose, maybe soaked on bread or biscuit.

"It must stink. Do they like it?"

"That is the clever part. It smells of…nothing. Tastes of nothing. You wouldn't know you taking it. Always kept it handy, just in case, you know…"

"No mum, I don't know. What ?! You gonna kill Mikey?"

"Don't be stupid, girl, I kill his mice. I know where they are. Under loose floorboards. But think about it. We help your Mikey with the micey, we get to look under the floor without him suspecting. We find his stash. THEN we poison him."

"MUM!!"

"Only joking. Let's go."

The two women didn't wait for an answer to their knock, they just strode into 31a like they owned the place – which, technically, they did. Mike Jones spun round in shock as they entered. Ludmilla was so focused on the bottle of poison and Rosie engrossed in trying to ascertain the whereabouts of Joe Nowak, neither of them noticed Jones sweating and holding his hands strangely behind his back.

"Excuse me, what do you think…" he tried to say, but Ludmilla cut him off.

"I bring poison, for the vermin. We must catch now before they take over, I haf seen it, believe me, in Kherson. I was working at bank, yes, and mices, they get into the safe and 'poof', all the money is shredded. Wouldn't want your nice suits to go the same way, Mr Jones. Now, let me see, I think there is a loose floorboard…."

Ludmilla made to get down to her knees, but Jones grabbed the bottle suddenly, distorting his arms to keep the bundles of notes stashed behind his back. With his hands now full, he brought his legs into action.

"Out. OUT! Both of you, leave me in peace." And with that he shepherded the two women skillfully like they were errant sheep– he was Welsh after all – out of his room into the corridor, slamming the door behind them with his other foot. He put the bottle of poison on the shelf beside the radio and returned to his chair in the alcove.

Out in the corridor, Rosie wasn't coping with the stress of it all.

"Great, Mum, now what??

"Now we watch, spy, see what he does."

"And how, pray do we do that, double O sodding 6 and a half?"

"Keyhole. On your knees. You're getting good at that." Before Rosie could remonstrate or let loose the rising bile of invective she wanted to hurl at her mother, she found herself spun round and thrust down onto her knees. She put her eye to the keyhole and winced as her expensive Russian Eyelash Extensions caught in the brass plate. Her eye roved around the room but for some reason she couldn't see Mike Jones anywhere. She was about to stand up when she saw something that made her snap back her head, ripping the extension painfully from her eyelash.

"Shiiiiiiiit" she cursed and looked again. She wasn't mistaken. Joe Nowak was creeping out of the kitchen, carrying a glass box. Where the hell was Mike?

The Southern Belles outside on Torrance Avenue had struck up again their cacophonous racket of clashing rhythms and melodies, with the bandleader yelling instructions from the front. They seemed to be stuck in limbo outside the house. Their noise seemed a perfect counterpoint to the unfolding silent drama taking place in the flat.

Rosie watched in horror as Joe put down the box onto a chair, then jump back in alarm as he found the dead mouse on the table.

"What the hell are you up to, you sneaky ugly git" muttered Rosie under her breath, as she watched Joe crouch down, pop up again, like he was both hiding and trying to catch someone unawares. Her bafflement was short lived as her mother yanked her to her feet. She was holding a bottle of wine.

"Here. Take this. Get in there and schmooze him. Find the money, yes?" And without hesitating Ludmilla leant passed her and knocked at the door.

Rosie spun round to find herself face to face with Joe Nowak. Joe was holding the dead mouse aloft so it was right in her eye line, just as she raised the bottle of wine in greeting. In a bizarre Bognor stand-off, which is nothing like it's more menacing Mexican version, Joe grabbed the wine just as Rosie grabbed the mouse, at which point Joe – embarrassed to be so close to the woman who had so hideously deflowered him earlier – slammed the door.

"Arrgh" grunted Rosie. Not knowing what to do, or what the actual fuck was going on, she scurried back to her flat to face the wrath of her mother. And dispose of the mouse.

LUCY'S TESTIMONY cont'd.

"So no joy then for Joe?"

"Not at this point no, not in the kitchen. He was staggered to find the mouse had returned, which really fused his poor brain. I mean, how...how did that happen? It wasn't the snake, obviously. What were those women playing at? And then he was perplexed to be given a bottle of wine by Rosie. He didn't know how to respond; he's not experienced in these things? He didn't know if it was a come-on, an apology or what it was. He just shut the door on her, he said. Didn't know what to say. He remembered seeing a corkscrew in the kitchen so went off to find it – poor Joe. Hadn't heard of screw tops."

MR JONES

"I got some of it stashed away in the vent. The racket from that band outside was doing my head in. Literally. Banging headache, not so nauseous. So I stepped down with still a sizeable amount in my hands and sort of gave up. I thrust what I had left behind the radio cassette thing. Not much of a hiding place, but then

I realized, I didn't need a hiding place – I was leaving today! And what was this with the poison, daft cow? If there are mice here I'm gunna nuke the little bastards. Where did I leave it...?...oh yes, on the mantlepiece. I sit at the table and try to decipher the label till I realise it's handwritten in Russian. Not my strong point. I was thinking of lying down again when my blood ran cold. There, on the table. A bottle of wine, right there, pride of place. First the mouse, then the money, now this. Those women. Had they been in, just now? Did they see me at the vent in the alcove? I had checked way back when I first moved in, you can't see the alcove if you've a mind to peer through the keyhole. Did they just waltz in unnoticed? Mikey boy, you are losing control of the situation. You need to get a grip, find out what they know. You need to take the initiative. Let's get that Rosie back over here, ply her with drink, see what she says. I need an excuse. Ah! Clean glasses. For all their shitty flat in this shitty town, if there's one thing I would say about the Shatalovas it's that they never skimp on the finer details. Fashion, perfume. They've probably got a set of Baccarat Crystal glasses over there. Let's go over there and see if she'll join me for a glass or two. I'll take the bottle by way of temptation.

LUCY'S TESTIMONY cont'd

He found the corkscrew but didn't get to use it. He came back in, he said, picked up the bottle and tried to force the corkscrew in but it wouldn't go. So he checked the bottle and was horrified to discover those women – probably that cow Rosie – had come in and taken the wine and replaced it with a bottle of weird Russian poison. He could make out the poison symbol but none of the words. Why would they do that? What's wrong with these people? Joe was just a simple soul, never hurt a fly, wanted to be everybody's friend. There he was, in a strange country, all alone, and he thinks people are trying to kill him. It was all too much. He thinks he just passed out on his bed…. sorry…. can we take a break?

ROSIE

Rosie was having a crisis. When she imagined her future, her adult life starting once she reached the age of 21, it didn't involve running around a dingy basement flat in Bognor Regis with a dead mouse dangling from her beautifully manicured hand. It didn't involve having to wine, dine and bed a scrawny man old enough to be her father, or then have to fellate a simpleton with a mis-shapen head. She was becoming hysterical.

"Mum, I've had it, really, I've had it. They're both in there, Mum, you get that. It's over. They will have met and now they'll be coming over here and…and…"

Ludmilla slapped her daughter sharply across the face. Empathetic parenting, Ukrainian style.

"Ach, stop your whinging. What, you scared? Of those two? Get a grip, you a Shatalova or what? We Shatalova women, we eat men like that for breakfast…"

"I just did, both of them, one of them…literally, at breakfast" wailed Rosie.

"We wrap those two round our fingers, yes? If it comes to it, we choose, you understand, we choose Mr Jones. So we lose the double rent, big deal, we know Mr Jones is rich. A plum for the plucking."

There was a gently tap at the door. The women froze.

"You answer, mum" said Rosie, tremulously. Ludmilla was standing in the doorway to her bedroom. She took one step back and shut the door. Rosie was about to remonstrate when there was a slightly more insistent tap.

"That sounds like Joe…. I can handle Joe" thought Rosie, so she went to the front door and slowly opened it.

Mike Jones was leaning against the door frame with a wry smile on his face. He held up the bottle of wine.

"What's this, hair of the dog? Or an invitation?" he asked quietly, looking intensely into her eyes. Rosie shuffled from one foot to another, glancing nervously over his shoulder trying to spot Joe Nowak. A sudden terrible thought flashed through her mind, and she immediately scanned Mike's clothes for signs of blood trauma. He mis-interpreted the look.

"I was thinking, seeing as I'm feeling a bit better, and having taken the day off…. seems a shame to waste it. You got any glasses?"

"Erm…right, yes, yes! I'll just get them." Rosie turned away, her mind flying about trying to settle on a workable plan. Best to get him into the flat then Mum can sort out Joe. Yes, that would be best. She got to the kitchen, grabbed the best glasses (Baccarat Crystal no less) and called him in. Silence. She went out and saw him disappearing up the corridor to 31a. Shit!

Rosie dashed after him and caught up just as he opened the door. He stepped in, smiling back at her, and waved her in. She stepped in like she was crossing a minefield. No sign of Joe as far as she could make out, but Mike's body was masking half of the room, so she couldn't see what he was doing in the alcove, or the bed. Had Joe gone for walk? Was he in the toilet? She looked about her, desperate for some evidence of Joe's existence.

"You ok? You seem nervous. Not like you. Here, give me the…oh, very nice. Crystal."

"No no, I'm fine. You?" she answered, like a trembling virgin on her first date. She handed over the glasses.

"Oh, I'm fine. How about some music, eh?"

He reached over to the radio and switched it on. The room was filled with the sound of the snake charmer.

"What the…. where the hell did that come from….?" Mike angrily pressed the radio button and the smooth tones of Marvin Gaye seeped into the room.

"Perfect" said Mike, smiling. "'Sexual Healing'. Right, I'll just grab a corkscrew."

"There's one there…on the floor by the table."

Jones stared down at the floor and then back at Rosie. A shadow of confusion passed across his face, and for a moment, the couple just stared at each other.

"Righto, yes, ok, well then." He stooped and grabbed the corkscrew then looked at the bottle.

"It's a screw-top."

"Is it…oh yes. South African."

"So…. why did I get a corkscrew?…I have no memory of getting a corkscrew."

"Well, last night was pretty epic…" She said. He was pouring out the wine.

"Here we go. Cheers". He handed her a glass, and Mike Jones took a sip just as Rosie glanced to her right and saw the prone body of Joe Nowak lying on the bed, holding the bottle of poison in his hand. He started to stir. Without thinking, Rosie threw her wine over Mike just as his head tipped back.

"Oh my God, I'm so sorry, I thought we were chinking."

"What!... what are you doing?"

"I'm so sorry, babes, I'm so clumsy. Here, let's go into the Kitchen, there should be a towel or something" and with that she grabbed his glass, put both onto the table and bundled Mike Jones into the Kitchen just as Joe roused himself.

WHAT THE DOG SAW

Dog had been watching the unfolding events in the room, fascinated to be learning so much about human behavior. For as long as he could remember, the activity in this room had been a daily round of clockwork episodes that brought him a level of certainty and thus warmth. But this last hour was very confusing. The Thin Man and the Woman That Smelt Strange were in the room and the Nice Man was lying on the bed. Dog was concerned the man's breathing was very shallow, but then he roused himself from the bed, just as the couple disappeared into the room where the Food Lived. Dog could hear gentle music, rhythmic, not unpleasant on the ears.

The Nice Man got to his feet – he seemed unsteady – but found himself swaying to the music and then – most strangely – dancing to it. Clearly not feeling himself, the Nice Man stopped dancing and looked about him, very confused. He noticed he had a bottle in his hand, which he threw onto the bed as if it had burnt him. The Nice Man then started to panic – Dog noticed the man's breathing increase, his blood flow flooding his body. Maybe he had remembered the snake, or that paper stuff that seemed to upset him so much. The man looked wildly about him, settling his gaze upon the wine, now open on the table. The Man picked the bottle up and suddenly sped out of the room, taking the wine with him.

Immediately the Woman That Smelt Strange came in from the Room where the Food Lived, carrying a piece of clothing – Dog recognized it as the shirt of the Thin Man. She was wafting the material about looking around her for something. She stood at the bottom of the bed and stared at where the Nice Man had been lying. She picked up the brown bottle and dropped it, then turned back to the table. Looking about her, Dog noticed something in her eyes which he recognized immediately. Fear. A memory flitted through his canine brain, his…. mother?……making it clear, 'never show another animal you're scared.' But this woman – she was very scared. She dashed back into the Food Room. Dog could see through the open front door of the flat down the corridor - a perfect vantage point. There he saw the Nice Man talking animatedly with the Woman Who Looked Strange. He was waving the bottle about, and then the Woman Who Looked Strange grabbed him and tried to pull him into her flat, but the Nice Man fought her off and rushed back into his room and shut the door.

The wine bottle was placed on the table, then the Nice Man stood still and thought for a moment, then seemed to make a decision. He went to the corner of the room where the loose floorboard was, behind the table, got onto his knees and lifted the board. Dog immediately knew what was happening. The Nice Man had remembered the Snake, so was getting another mouse. He knelt over the hole, stock still, like a hunting cat. Or a dog.

ROSIE

Mike had washed himself off sufficiently in the kitchen and wanted to resume the drinking so Rosie, realizing she couldn't delay the inevitable any longer, led him out into the main room. She was looking left and right but Joe seemed to have gone. Breathing a sigh of relief she turned, refilled the glasses and handed one to the shirtless Mike Jones. She started to sway her hips to the music to rekindle the moment though for the life of her she couldn't remember what she was doing there in the room in the first place. Her natural feminine instinct – to befriend a threat – led her to move in on Mike, but in doing so her eyeline fell upon Joe Nowak, crouched on the floor behind the table staring into a hole in the floor. Without any attempt at pretense Rosie threw her glass of wine straight into Mike's face. Before he could remonstrate she noiselessly bundled the poor man out of the flat, grabbing his shirt from the chair and into the corridor. She slammed the flat door behind her and pushed Mike into the toilet. He exploded as she tried to shut him in.

"Fuck a priest, what the hell are you playing at? Are you completely mental?" Unable to explain any more, and with no capacity left for over-wrought emotion, Rosie mumbled an apology, shut him in the toilet and burst into tears.

With mascara cascading down her face like a Mexican landslide after heavy rain, she turned to go back towards her room, but was met by her mother.

"What's the matter, crybaby? You big girl now, you 21, yes?"

"Oh mum, just shut up. I literally have no idea what is going on."

"Then we find out." Ludmilla pushed Rosie aside and knelt at the keyhole.

"Ah ha! Got you, you useless piece of dog shit."

Ludmilla barged into 31a, followed by the snuffling Rosie. Standing in the middle of the room stroking a large mouse was Joe Nowak. Caught red-handed, Joe thrust the timorous beastie into his trouser pocket. Mouse, being suddenly thus confined, scrabbled for freedom, causing Joe to break into a strange dance of discomfort. It wriggled! It bit!! He pulled the mouse out and immediately lost control of it. He juggled it comically into the air, caught it and dashed its brains out on the table. Only then did he realise what Ludmilla was doing. Whilst preoccupied with the temporary welfare of one mouse, Ludmilla had grabbed the poison bottle from the bed and was sprinkling a generous and deadly dose into the gap created by the absent floorboard. Joe stood and watched, aghast at her callousness. She finished her work, kicked the floorboard shut, plonked the bottle on the table and turned to Joe.

"Mister Nowak, you take us for fools? You know the rules. No pets. No pets, no dogs and definitely no filthy mices. You clear, yes? Now, you sleep now. Work tonight."

Ludmilla marched out of the flat, dragging Rosie behind her. In the corridor she met Mike Jones, pulling on his damp shirt, and rubbing a towel over his face.

"Ah, you feelink better Mister Jones?"

"No, I bloody don't. I feel wretched as it happens."

"Well, you'll live. Just a touch of man-flu no doubt. Best get off to work, eh? Shall I get you another shirt?"

"No, you bloody won't. I know what you're up to, you two. I can see your game and I tell you, I'm on to you. Now piss off, I'm going to get some shut eye." And before Ludmilla could intervene anymore, Mike Jones threw the towel over his head, pushed passed the two women, opened his door, and disappeared into his flat.

"Now what, mum? sniffled Rosie. "What we gunna do?"

"We do nothink. We let them sort this mess out and when the time comes…we act. Now though, I think a drink is in order."

"It's 9.30 in the morning!"

"So what!? Who are you now, the Prosecco Police? Come, my lovely girl…"

And with that, Ludmilla led Rosie back to the safety of their flat and the comforting lift of a few bubbles for brunch.

WHAT THE DOG SAW.

Dog continued to be intrigued. He had never seen humans behaving like this before, and his previous master had some peculiar habits. He had once witnessed his owner nailing another man's hand to a table. The noise was terrible, but the blood was a treat. Dog watched events unfold, saw The Nice Man fetch another mouse and then The Fat Woman Who Looked Strange came in. He watched as the mouse was dispatched, licking his lips just in case it came his way – any meal was something to be grateful for, frankly. But the Looking Strange Woman then left after pouring something into the Mouse House, and The Nice Man looked very upset. He turned the music off, stuffed the dead mouse into one of the glasses and fell onto his bed, curling himself up into a ball, and in no time Dog saw the Nice Man's breath even out as he fell asleep. But then the Thin Man came in with a towel over his head. He backed up to the bed, dropped the towel on the floor and lay down sideways on the bed, his back to the other man. Very soon Dog saw his breath also even out. Dog whimpered. Both the Nice Man and the Thin Man were asleep on the same bed.

PART FOUR

'Whether we fall by ambition,
blood or lust
Like diamonds we are cut with
our own dust'

Webster (Duchess of Malfi)

NOVEMBER 3, MID MORNING

LULU GOLD

Smoking a cheroot and sipping a 75-year-old Mortlach single malt, Lulu gold stared out over the grey English Channel from her private room. So many hues of grey, between the sea and the sky. But her mood was black, no white impinging on her fury to lessen its intensity. That she had lost Nosmo to what transpired was a deadly snakebite was hard enough to take. But the news from Mayfair this morning was more than she could stomach. An estimated £2.2m was missing. The accountant had taken advantage of her when she strived so hard to be a fair and equitable employer. Two years previously, Jones had debts from a lifestyle not matching his income as an accountant with a water company. He had racked up large sums with a London-based private casino, run as a subsidiary money-laundering racket by Gold. Mr Jones had no way of paying off that which he owed. Gold suggested the arrangement, that he works for her, since she had some hold over him. Jones was unaware Lulu Gold was so closely connected to the Casino, and tragically presumed the South Coast outfit would be a soft touch. But Gold had a way of letting her employees know what was expected of them, and what the consequences would be should they ever cross her. And yet. And yet…..

Lulu Gold savoured the moment as she thought about what she was going to do to Mike Jones when he arrived this morning. She ran through the options, lived the possible moments of terrified realization flashing across his face, bleeding out through his eyes, screaming from his throat. Inflicting pain had its own peculiar pleasure, but for Gold the prize was the psychological collapse, witnessing a human being, the alpha species of the last 500,000 years realizing they were mere prey and were about to die.

There was a gentle tap at the door.
"Come."
Milo eased open the door and stuck his head in.
"It's 9.30 and he's just called in sick."

Gold rolled the ice around the glass. Then she drained the last drop, stubbed out her cheroot, swiveled her chair slowly back and forth.
"We've tracked his phone and his briefcase. Both still at Torrance Road."

"If he was out on the town last night, maybe he is poorly. I'll make a visit. Bring him in."

"Very good, Ma'am. Want some company?"

"No, I'll be fine. You've got the architect meeting at the Itchenor house. Make sure he knows we want to move at least 3 mill through this deal. It'll be a cash deal, untraceable."

Milo whistled softly.

"£3 million? For that little bungalow? You don't think that's pushing it?"

"Make it a big bungalow. Top spec on everything. Milo, never underestimate the stupidity of a minted yachtie. I once sold a 1 bed flat in West Wittering to some Ad agency surfer dude who needed somewhere warm to change in and out of his wetsuit. £850,000. When you're pursuing the dream, the sky's the limit. So long as it's instagrammable, they'll pay. Look at Vee Dubs. Mechanically challenged rust buckets. Going for thousands.

"I had a VW camper, early days. Shifting product out of Morocco."

"Really Milo? Can't see you slumming it in a camper. What did you pay for it?"

"Back then? 2 Thou."

"See. You should've held on to it. Worth 30k at least now. Get the Merc ready."

Milo, knowing the conversation had been ended, slipped out and shut the door. Gold opened the top

drawer of the smart George II mahogany Partners Desk
and stared at the tools of her trade

THE DREAM OF JOE NOWAK.

Joe is standing at the doorway to his stepparent's
bedroom, in a dilapidated farmhouse on the outskirts
of the village in Poland. Sun filters in through the
ragged net curtain, the window is open, and he can
smell cherry and apple blossom, mingling with the
pungent odours of animals in the farmyard. Silence.
No coughing from his father or grumbling mother.
Joe feels the silence viscerally, an absence that makes
him tremble. It causes him to feel like he's losing his
connection with the earth, loosing his moorings from
the bankside and drifting out onto the canal. And
now he's in the little rowing skiff he was told his real
father used to fish from on hazy summer afternoons.
Joe peers into the green slow-flowing water and sees
his father floating by two foot down and face up. Joe's
father gives him a thumbs up and a toothy smile. Joe
feels reassured by this but then notices the four Drab
brothers coming towards him on the towpath. They're
carrying sticks and stones and he knows they mean to
hurt him. They start throwing rocks at him and calling
him cruel names. His panic upends the boat and he's
in the water. But when he resurfaces he's in the Drab
kitchen at lunchtime. Magdalena is there in a wedding

dress but is ignoring him, whilst the four brothers are looking daggers at him. Mother and Father Drab stare at Joe with undisguised loathing. Joe starts to lay the table, fetching crockery, cutlery, and napkins, setting new flowers in the vases. But as he walks past a brother, he feels a sharp pain in his leg. He has been stabbed. Another brother leans over and sticks a vegetable paring knife into his shoulder. Not wanting to be a burden on the family Joe continues the meal preparation while trying not to bleed too profusely and thus incur further Drab wrath. But another brother stabs him in the back and the fourth brother sticks a carving knife into Joe's stomach. He's feeling faint but realizes the grandfather clocks needs winding so takes the key, opens the face, and inserts the key. Winding up the pendulum he starts to find it hard to keep himself upright, so he leans against the clock. His weight topples the family's pride and joy and time itself crashes to the floor. As he falls he reaches out to steady himself on the table and succeeds only in stripping the tablecloth from the table, causing the heirloom crockery to smash with a shocking finality onto the hard flagstone floor. He lies, broken, in a pool of his own blood. Staring across the floor he is shocked to see his mother, his dead mother, slowly disappearing into the mouth of huge snake, curled up under the vast Drab family dresser. Joe whimpers and tries to wake up.

THE DREAM OF MIKE JONES

Jones sits at vast desk, so huge he can hardly see over the top of it. The room is windowless, featureless, but sounds from elsewhere bleed into the space. Screams, moans, babbling voices. A harsh shade-less bulb hangs above him, and he stares at a plain wooden door opposite. On the back of the door hangs a picture, a wonderful photograph of an azure sky above turquoise water and a white sandy beach. Palm trees sway in the light breeze. Why are they moving, it's a photograph, isn't it? Or is it a strange window? Scantily clad women amble across the sand, beckoning him to join them. In the distance is a bar and seated at the bar he can see the faces of his old mates from Cardiff. They're waving at him, calling him over, laughing and joshing.

He looks down. The desk is empty. He feels dread at the emptiness of the desk. He should be doing something, but he doesn't know what it is. To his left he sees a drawer slightly open, and inside he can see the edge of an accounts ledger. If he can only get the ledger out and onto the desk, open it and see what it says then he knows he'll be alright. But he can't move. His arms are like lead, and no amount of effort will lift them. He sweats, the room starts to spin, he feels himself lose control of his bladder. He knows he's in trouble, that there will be terrible consequences, but he can't help himself. He hears feet approaching, strange feet, tip-tapping on the wooden floor. They stop at the door. A scrabbling sound then the door swings open. Jones opens his mouth to scream but no sound will come out. A huge mouse stands in the doorway, monstrously up on its back legs. The mouse pulls back its lips to reveal two vast yellow front teeth. Its mouth opens and closes and it seems to be sniffing the air. The beast notices Jones, puny, behind the desk. The mouse fixes Jones with its glinting beady eyes then drops down onto all fours. Jones loses sight of it. He wants to move but his legs won't work, they're no longer his legs, they're his and not his, but he can still feel…. feel the brush of fur against his leg, the first tentative exploratory bites with those terrible yellow teeth. Jones screams for help, but his voice is like a dry retch, painful and unproductive. Then an obliterating pain as he feels the whole of one calf is ripped off the bone. Jones screams and tries to wake up.

WHAT LUDMILLA AND ROSIE DID NEXT.

The Shatalova women busied themselves in 31b for a while, on tenterhooks, not knowing what was transpiring next door. Ludmilla was brusque and working herself up for a fight, girding her considerable loins for the anticipated set-to. Rosie's nerves were shredded and got a double dose of no sympathy from her mother.

Rosie still worried about what people thought about her, whereas Ludmilla had had that facility beaten out of her over many years of hard grafting in post-Soviet Ukraine. Finally, the tension in the flat got too much for Rosie.

"Mum, we gotta know what's what, are they killing each other, shagging, playing cards and planning our murder?"

"More to the point, where is all the money?"

"You don't know…."

"Ach of course he has more money. You think he comes home from work just one day with a case full? I reckon it's under the floor. You saw Joe, he had a board up, maybe Mr Jones has many boards."

"Well, I can't wait no longer. I'm gunna have a peek."

Rosie left the flat and stood outside 31a. First she listened at the door, then crouched down and peered through the keyhole. Then she grinned. Ludmilla appeared at her side with a jemmy in her hand.

"Whassup? What you see?"

They're both asl…. MUM! What you doing with that thing?"

"Shhh girl, not going to brain them…. not yet anyhow, but maybe if we get the chance, you know, look under the floor?"

"Well, they're both asleep. On the same bed."

"Perfect. They sleep the sleep of the dead. Iron is hot. We strike." And before Rosie could stop her, Ludmilla opened the door and stepped into the bedroom.

The two men were indeed asleep, back-to-back, both with their knees drawn up. Ludmilla and Rosie tiptoed up to the bed and looked closer. They looked at each other and pulled an 'Aw, sweet' face. Rosie pointed down at Mike – he had Joe's soft toy duck clasped in his arms. Maybe sensing a change in the room, both men suddenly readjusted. They both turned themselves over, so they were now facing each other. Ludmilla, unable to restrain herself, gingerly lifted Joe's arm by the cuff and placed it gently on Mr Jones's shoulder. Rosie pulled an angry face at her, so Ludmilla signalled to Rosie to get onto her knees. The two women then proceeded to crawl about the flat, tap-tapping on the floorboards to locate a loose one. Rosie stopped. Was this board loose? She beckoned her mother over. Ludmilla, in a scene from a bad pantomime, heaved herself across the floor on all fours. She tapped the floor. She tapped again. Possibly. She tapped once more, louder and harder this time, and with the jemmy. It was loud enough to summon Satan to the gates of hell. Both men jerked awake from their terrifying dreams, sitting bolt upright. The two women, unseen, jumped to their feet, smacked into each other before Ludmilla bundled them into the nearest hiding place – the wardrobe. Lucky for them

Joe hung nothing up, so the space was empty. They huddled in, keeping the door open by a sliver to watch – and hear – what progressed.

Both men momentarily sat up, rubbed their eyes, and when Joe slapped his thigh Jones jumped out of his skin, followed immediately by a yelp from Joe.

"What the….. Christ!…. who the hell are you… what are you doing in my bedroom?" spat out Mike, leaning away from Joe.

Joe looked indignant. His English was ok, and he understood the profanities. "Your room? My room!"

"No mate, my room. How d'ya get in, fer Chris' sakes? Clear off!"

Both men were standing either side of the bed, unsure whether they faced a crazed lunatic or a sad fool. When one went left, the other went left, keeping the bed perfectly between them. At the same time, they were rubbing their eyes, both prematurely woken from deep sleep and unsettling dreams.

"If it is your room, why you holding daffy?" said Joe, pointing to his fluffy duck he liked to cuddle up to at night. Mike looked down at the toy he was still clutching. He flung it across the floor.

"I don't care…I…. just get out!" he shouted at Joe.

"But this is my flat. My duvet. My pictures. Look, my clothes in drawers." Joe was up, running about the room, pointing out everything that was his. Mike followed him with mounting incredulity…and panic. Struck by a thought, he opened the front door and pointed triumphantly at the '31a' sign.

"There you go, chum. 31a. I live at 31a. Now scram before I call the police. Maybe I should call immigration!"

"But I live 31a too" squealed Joe. "And I here legally, yes? EU, remember?"

"There's only one way to sort this. Let's ask the lovely ladies down the corridor."

"Of course! Good idea, we ask Rosie and Mrs…."

"Let's go. After you." Mike held the door open to allow Joe to stride purposefully and innocently out of the flat. As soon as he had left, Mike slammed the door and locked it.

"….and stay out!" shouted Jones at the door.

Joe was furious, and felt very foolish at such an easy deception, but was struck by a clever idea.

Inside 31a Jones was also struck by an idea, a very unpalatable one. If this man had access to his flat, then maybe…..!! Jones rushed to the alcove and grabbed a chair on the way. Throwing it against the wall he propelled himself up and ripped the vent from the wall. So engrossed was he that he missed the wardrobe door creak open another inch and the wide-eyed gaze of the Shatalovas fall upon his beloved millions. All present and correct, and momentarily reassured, he shut the vent as the women pulled the wardrobe to a close. Jones stood for a moment and looked around him. He was in his flat, but that wasn't his duvet cover. Those weren't his pictures nor the clothes on the floor. He felt his stomach flutter, a rush of unhelpful chemicals coursing through his body. Rising panic left him momentarily frozen to the spot. Think, man think!

Mike rushed to the door and threw it open, intending to confront the man with the funny shaped head. But he was gone. Left and right, no sight of him. He tiptoed up to 31b and listened intently at the door. Was he in there? Plotting? Hearing nothing he resolved to burst in on them but just as he grabbed the door handle, he heard a door slam. His door. 31a.

"Shitty bollocks" he spat out and careened into his front door. It was locked.

"Listen here you worthless piece of shit, open the door NOW" he yelled at Joe.

Joe had been clever. He had gone out onto the road, pushed open the street-level window and dropped in onto the bed. His bed.

"This my flat, you bad man. You go away now, thank you."

There was silence. Nothing moved, no noise. Joe withdrew his key, knelt and peered through the keyhole, just as Mike jammed his key hard into hole, smacking Joe in the eye. Joe fell back as Mike burst into the room, but with such force and physical venom that momentum carried him straight across the room and into the kitchen. Joe chased after him, and they immediately set about each other with tools and implements that until now had been completely useless to them, since none of the tools were required in the preparation of Pot Noodles.

Ludmilla and Rosie chose this moment to make a swift exit from the wardrobe, but Rosie's dash for the door was halted by a yank from her mother, who pointed violently towards the vent. Rosie tried to silently remonstrate with her, but Ludmilla gripped her arm like she used to strong-arm a punter into the alley. She grabbed a chair with her free hand and slung it against the wall under the vent. She was in the throes of trying to unscrew the vent when the two men entered the bedroom.

Joe had a colander on his head, Mike a saucepan. They were both armed with long-handled implements – Joe a ladle and Mike a fish slice. Both men, being neither sporty, naturally aggressive or used to scrapping, were duelling most ineffectively, making more noise than causing harm. The overall effect was one of pure comedy, though of course neither man found anything remotely funny about the situation. They circumnavigated the room like a silent film brawl, lunging and retreating, whilst sweating and swearing. If there was a soundtrack it would be the great key change in Ravel's Bolero, both resembling crazed percussionists trying to outdo each other. They both became aware of the two women at about the same time, the great battle quickly petering out as if the conductor had dropped his baton.

"What the hell are you two doing up there?" asked Mike, although he was fully cognisant of the answer.

"Rosie, please, tell this man, this my flat, he must go, yes? You tell him now?"

Ludmilla stepped down from the chair, supported by her daughter. Ludmilla had a swagger that Rosie didn't feel so she just watched her mum rather than catch the eye of either man.

"Right then gents, maybe you should sit down, and I explain. Everything."

"I don't feel like sitting, thank you very much" sneered Mike.

"Suit yourself. It's like this. Mister Jones, you take the flat last year, you answer the advert in Bognor Observer, yes? But you out every day, like clockwork, never miss a day. All day the flat sits there empty. We read, there is a housing shortage, people need rooms to stay.. Bloody second homeowners, they take everything. Then we meet Joe, fishing on the canal and sleeping in a tent. He's Polish, he feeling sad from very bad marriage and he needs a home. But he works nights. So I see a solution to reach out helping hand, understand?

Good Samaritan. We offer Joe a room during the day
for sleeping and you, Mister Jones for the night. You
both work so hard, never a day off, it works fine. A few
hiccups. You remember, Mister Jones you had weekend
off, yes? We thought it was over, but you went away
to London. Had a good time, I bet. And you, Joe,
at Christmas you went home to see your sister Lucy.
This saves our bacon. But now, well, the cookie has
crumbled, and we are where we are. I have a solution,
of course. Since neither of you was any the wiser until
just now, I suggest we can come to an arrangement.
Maybe we reduce rent, 5% all round, by way of ...."

"Absolutely not. This is my flat, I live here, I was
here first, so this gormless idiot needs to pack his things
and sod off, get me?" Jones was furious.

Ludmilla tried to wheedle but Jones shut her down
immediately.

"Get him out. Now!"

Joe had been trying to follow proceedings. He
couldn't make out all the details, but he realised the
game was up when he saw both women and Mike
looking at him.

"Rosie? What is this meaning?"

"Sorry Joe. Grab yer things. You need to go."

"Go where? I live here, no? Nowhere else."

"Joe. Seriously. Out." Rosie wasn't having her heart
strings plucked. She turned her back on him.

Joe, not knowing what to do, and finding history repeating itself in the cruellest of fashions, just walked out of the door. Rosie followed him trying to apologise, and Ludmilla went after her just in case her daughter was too soft and relented on the expulsion of the now-worthless Joe Nowak. They watched him disappear down towards the beach and saw him pull out his phone.

"He'll be calling his clever sister the big baby" scoffed Ludmilla. "Come on, girl, let's get back to our future. We've hit the big time!"

Rosie turned back to the house and followed her mum's triumphant sashay down the steps. But she couldn't quite shake the feeling of foreboding she first felt about 30 hours previously.

SLOW JOE

WEST SUSSEX POLICE, BOGNOR DIVISION:
INVESTIGATION INTO THE UNEXPLAINED
DEATH OF JOE NOWAK;
The concluding part of Lucy Nowak's testimony.

He wasn't making any sense, just sobbing and sniffing. I managed to get him to calm down and he told me everything that had happened, which I just told you. That was everything. He explained about the trick those women played upon him, and he was so upset. He doesn't understand how people can be so cruel, because you see, he is so nice. Always has been. An innocent, like a baby. This world was too cruel for him. He was crying and saying it was his fault. I was mad. I was, like, "How is it your fault, Joe, those women they are bitches" but he says no no no and starts wailing again. And then he starts to have a panic attack, I hear him, the snake and everything. I tell him "JOE! Go straight back. You tell them you pay rent, you have rights, you're in England, there are laws. And find bloody snake double quick". He stops crying now and he agrees he'll go back, but first he has seen the Kiosk is open so he gets an ice cream. In November! See what I mean, Detective? He's just a baby. Maybe he ate ice cream and wandered around Bognor for a while. At some point he must have gone back. What did they do to him, detective? You not tell us anything? I can take the truth….

Detective Supt Bovey tried to explain the ongoing and rather confusing nature of the unfolding events at 31 Torrance Avenue. He reassured Ms Nowak that when they had a clearer idea of what occurred, she'd be the first to know. Until then, they would have to keep Joe's body in the mortuary in case further analysis was needed.

MR JONES

"Those conniving bastards! All this time they've been ripping me off, and to be fair, that unfortunate bloke Joe. I feel quite sorry for him now. I saw him earlier when I came home this morning feeling God-awful.

Rosie must've waylaid him and, by the looks of things, screwed the poor sod. So, last night? Did she fancy me, or had they clocked my stash? Get real, Boyo, you're not exactly a catch without the cash. They knew. They've been playing me all along. And now they've chucked him out they think they've done me a favour, see! They'll be all over me like a Swansea Rash. I need to free myself from this situation, good and proper. Get them off my back, clear out the stash and head for the airport. If they know I've done a runner without them they're going to play nasty. Might even drop me in it with HER, Christ alive!

Right. Decision time. They'll be back in a tick. And the way out for me is on the table! This poison stuff looks lethal. And odourless. Probably won't kill them but might give me enough time to get into the air. There we go, a healthy dose into the wine bottle, swirl it around. Fantastic. Now. Music!

Radio 1 Xtra, not my normal choice, but it's upbeat enough to get a party started. Here we go, back in the room.

"Ladies, that was masterly! The way you dealt with that wanker, fair play to you, couldn't have handled it better myself!"

"Mike, you're a dark horse, ain't cha?" said Rosie, throwing herself onto the bed. Ludmilla accepted the proffered wine bottle from me and took a greedy swig.

"Come on, girl, you're 21 now, let's dance, celebrate!" said Ludmilla, starting to sashay around the floor.

"Yeah babes! Part-ay!" Rosie jumped up and grabbed the bottle. She threw back her head and suckled like a baby at the teat.

"Whoah, save me some, Rosie girl" laughed her mother as she took back the bottle. The two women linked arms and danced in front of me, and I'm just standing there watching, grinning like a madman.

"Come on, dance with us!" screamed Rosie above the beats. Why not, I thought, so I shimmed onto the make-shift dance floor and swung my hips. With an arm around the waist of each woman I spun them round in a giddy pirouette. The women screamed like dizzy kippers, the bottle of wine suddenly threatening to free itself from Rosie's grip and smash against a wall. I took it from her as she swung past and set it upon the table. They continued to shriek and twirl until they noticed bank notes falling around them like confetti. I had grabbed a stash of the cash on the shelf behind the radio and now stood on the bed, bouncing in time to the music, encouraging them like a demented DJ, flicking £50 notes into the air. The women jumped about, trying to catch as much as they could, stuffing the money into their bras. I couldn't stop myself laughing manically. The music, the money, the wine, all combined to drive the mood of the women into a bacchanalian excess, their dervish dance teetering on the edge of spinning out of control. But suddenly, like a jumping record, Rosie jerked to a stop.

"Hey Mum, I feel a bit shit, if I'm honest" said Rosie.

"You too? Me, I feel not good," said Ludmilla as she fell upon her daughter for support. "My guts feel wretched."

"Mum…it hurts…"

I stopped flicking the money and watched the two women. Wow. This wasn't what I was expecting, they were, like, literally dying before my eyes. What do I do? Call an ambulance? Explain that away, you idiot.

"Vlad…Vlad's poison…. he's…" blurted Ludmilla

"Mikey, what you done….? What you done? You've killed us….!!" Rosie was weeping and vomiting and holding her hands out to me imploring me to help. They had both fallen to the ground and were writhing in agony.

"Baboushka….." Ludmilla was weeping and trying to hug Rosie. "So sorry, this all my…. fault…"

I guess that Russian poison must be acid-based, because it looked like it burned through their guts in no time. They were coughing and spewing up blood, then bile, wailing and clawing at each other, trying to speak, until finally all that came out their lip-sticked mouths were bubbles. The bubbles popped into nothing, and they were gone.

I stopped bouncing and stared at them. They were locked in a death embrace, their faces pulled back in a rictus grin of …what? Pain? Shock? One last laugh at the futility of life….?

I had just killed two people. I thought it would just knock them out. I waited for the shock, the horror to kick in. But nothing. No guilt. Just…a sense of calm, of 'what next…? I was minted and stuck in basement hovel with two corpses in buggering-Bognor Regis. I'm in a sodding Coen Brothers film. This is the fourth instalment of Fargo. I need to move out of here sharpish.

I stepped down from the bed and switched the cheery pop music off. Enough of that rubbish. But the music is replaced by the howling of the dog outside. That fecking dog, what's its problem, eh? Barking like a mad one. That bloody dog has been the bane of my life. Into the kitchen, grab a bowl, and throw some bread in it, along with a little bit of the poison. That should do it.

I get up onto the bed and open the window. The dog nearly falls in in his fury but when I put the bowl on the windowsill for him, he wolfs it down double quick. Now, time to clean up and head on out. I take the poison bottle into the kitchen, turn the taps on full and swirl the poison down the drain. I can hear the dog growling and whimpering, then a thrashing sound and silence. I let the taps run to clear the poison. For some reason I start to sing. Loud. Release of pressure I guess. *'Hen Wlad Fy Nhadau'*. Old Land of My Fathers. Perfect. I switch the taps off and head back to clear out the stash from the vent.

LULU GOLD

She parked up and watched the house. First a funny looking man came out, followed by two women, one young, one older, both overly made-up. The man seemed dejected and lost, wandered this way and that before heading towards the sea. The two women were laughing and pointing at him.

"God, I hate Bognor" she thought, as she watched the two women disappear back into the basement flat. She waited a few more minutes then opened the Mercedes door and stepped out. She could hear tinny dance music coming from the flat, laughing, shouting, and clapping. Then just the music. Then silence. She stopped as the dog, lying against the street level window started to howl crazily. She watched as the window opened and the dog disappeared inside. She tapped the Beretta with a silencer in her inner pocket of her leather knee-length coat and stepped across the road to No 31a. Down the steps. The door was slightly ajar. She peaked in.

"Christ Almighty" she swore as she opened the door further. The two women, a moment ago laughing and jeering so full of life on the street, now lay stretched out, covered in…. what was that? Blood, puke, bile…. and money. Her money.

She could hear taps running in the kitchen beyond. And strong, strident singing in a strange language. She trod lightly into the room, turned, and shut the door. There was a key in the door, so she locked it and withdrew the key. She turned and surveyed the space. Childish pictures on the wall, a cartoon duvet cover. This was very different to the flat she was in earlier. And there was the dog, very much a dead dog, sprawled over the bed, blood dribbling from its mouth. Slightly perplexed but confident in the outcome, she sat herself down on the chair by the bed and pulled out the Beretta and laid it on her lap.

The taps were turned off, the singing ceased, and Mike Jones strode purposefully into the bedroom, drying his hands on a cloth. He skidded to a stop.

"Shiiii…. Miss Gold! Sorry, I didn't hear…." He petered out when he realised there were two dead bodies on the floor and Gold was holding a gun. This wasn't going to be a normal conversation.

"Sorry about today…. felt…. not right….and you…. here?"

"Mr Jones, I do believe I was explicitly clear about the consequences of playing with me, isn't that right?"

Mike nodded weakly, his eyes darting about, desperately searching for an out.

"So now what do we do, Mr Jones?"

"I.....give it back?"

"Excellent idea. All £2.4 million of it. Including this blood-stained lot on the floor. Every penny. What happened here?"

Mike opened his mouth to speak but she waves him away.

"You know what, I don't want to hear it, you and your sordid little peccadilloes with these two whores. I'll confess you're a mystery to me, Mr Jones, you're a right piece of work. Underneath that bland exterior lies a nasty little man. So. Where is it? Where have you hidden my money?"

"I.... what's...going to happen...?" asked Mike tremulously.

"I'll decide that in detail when I have my money back. But rest assured, none of it is good. You will be dead by tonight, but in how much pain depends on how you behave now. And if you tell me what you kept under the bed."

"Under...?"

"Yes. We visited you last night while you were out. Something bit Nosmo and now he's dead. I'd like to know about that. But first. The money."

"The…money" parroted Jones. He turned to the kitchen.

"It's in there."

"We looked in there."

"There's…. there's a secret compartment. 2 mill takes a lot of space."

"Mmmm. Ok. Show me."

Jones turned to the kitchen. He pushed open the door and stood aside to let her in. As she stepped over the threshold, Jones shoved her hard in the back, sending her sprawling onto the floor. He slammed the door and bolted across the room, but the door was locked. He fumbled in his pocket for his key but a blow to his back ripped open his left lung and shredded his liver. He spun round and saw Lulu Gold standing in the kitchen doorway pointing a gun at him. He was trying to process what had happened when he realised he was struggling to breathe. Then his legs started to give way.

"Come on you piece of shit, where is it hidden?" hissed Gold. Jones couldn't speak, but he staggered over to the table and sat down. He was gurgling.

"This is such a disappointment, Jones. I was going to have such fun with you. I've been playing around with a Dremel – you know, one of those craft tools, with different attachments. I managed to flail a man's skin off in 20 minutes. I'd have enjoyed that with you.

But no. You're done for. I'll get the boys round and we'll strip this place bare. Don't worry, we'll find it."

Jones had reached down and managed to pull his briefcase up onto the table. He clicked open the lid and let it fall back. Inside was still a considerable pile of rolled up 50's. Pathetically he tried to pick them up and put them in his pockets.

"Jones, you stupid moron, you really can't take it with you." Gold lifted the gun and dispatched the unfortunate Mike Jones with a bullet to the forehead. The bullet ripped through his prefrontal cortex, destroying all the mathematical skill he had accumulated, as well as the elaborate rationalisations he made these last two years. His pragmatic and adult brain thus destroyed; Jones enjoyed a fleeting – very fleeting - moment of pure emotion as all that was left to control him was his amygdala. His final nano-second of life was rich in teenage abandon, irrational joy, and optimism for the future.

Gold sighed. She was angry and frustrated, and now there was still work to do. She realised she might as well spend a few moments searching, so she picked up the bottle of wine, now half empty, and absent-mindedly swigged from it as she ambled around the flat. Not a bad wine, considering. She bent down to the two dead women and used the silencer to lift back their hair and observe their facial expressions. She stood, drank again, and then noticed the raised floorboard by the table. She put the bottle down and knelt beside the board. She was disturbed to see a large quantity of dead mice collected around the opening. This flat was weird.

She stood and immediately knew something was wrong. Terribly wrong.

"No no no…. no, not like this…. not here….. Jones you bastard…."

Gold was bent over in agony and still tried to make her way out of the room. She succeeded in getting the key from her pocket and opening the door. Blood started to fill her mouth as her insides turned to soup, but still she walked. Up the stairs and out into the grey Bognor morning. She stood, barely conscious, as seagulls screeched and wheeled above her. One foot, then another, she tried to walk towards the car. But that was too much for Lulu Gold. Massive organ failure did for her. She fell, face down, in front of the filthy window. As her life seeped out from her, her eyes focused into the room. Through the grime she saw an air conditioning vent, slightly askew. Barely visible, she could just make out bank notes, rolled and stuffed. Her money. Right in front of her. That's where the accountant had hidden it. It was always the accountant.

She stopped breathing.

WHAT THE SNAKE SAW

From his hidey hole, Pat had watched the unfolding drama with a reptilian disinterest. His flicking tongue sensed the change in certain chemical signals emanating from the humans. He sensed fear, panic, pain, anger. His vomeronasal organ, combined with the ability to hear through his jawbone gave Pat a pretty good picture of what was going on. He just lacked the ability to comprehend any of it or show any feelings for the actors in the drama.

He was now looking at 5 corpses. 4 humans and one canine. None were any good to him at all, though the dead mice would've been of interest if they hadn't given off such a revolting smell at the point of death. Something he hadn't encountered before, something chemical and stringent. Best avoid.

He was just settling back into sleep when the door opened and in walk Joe. He didn't know his name was Joe, but he knew very well who he was. This was the man who kept him imprisoned. This was the man who emanated a dreadful sound, a wailing noise whenever he wanted Pat to feed. Pat liked to catch his own food, to hunt, to allow himself some variety. This man, Joe kept him in the dark and fed him dusty, dead mice. Pat didn't like Joe. He observed and listened. Being a snake, he didn't understand any human language, so he didn't know Joe was speaking Polish.

"Oh my goodness…oh my…. oh my. But this is terrible. Rosie, what has happened to you, and your mother? Quite dead. And so much blood, oh my…. oh my! Who has done this terrible thing to you? And…. This man, the man in my flat, he's…. oh my…and the DOG!. No no no not the dog."

Pat watched as Joe travelled around the room, inspecting each corpse as he found them, crossing himself and whimpering in grief, until finally Joe just sat on the bed, nursing the dog, and rocking back and forth.

After a while he stopped rocking. Pat sensed a change in Joe.

"This is my fault. All my fault. It was the snake; he must've done this to all of them. They were having a drink, yes…a bottle of wine, then snake attacked. Killed the two women…. Rosie, she was so pretty… and then the dog. And this man. He has been bitten…. on his forehead. That is a big bite! I must…..I must…. I must ring Lucy, she'll…..but she'll…No! I can't. It'll kill her, she is so sweet and kind, and to know her brother is a mass murderer. It would kill her too. I must be strong. I must deal with this myself."

Pat watched Joe walk around the room for a while, then stop at his bed, where the dressing gown lay. It was a plain towelling robe with a flower embroidered over the breast. Joe pulled out the cord from the gown.

Pacing again, his eyes latched onto the only high point in the room where a noose may be attached. Muttering 'Magdalena' a few times, and crying, snivelling and sighing, Joe dragged a chair over to the air vent. He stood on the chair and tied the gown cord around his neck. On the other end he fashioned a simple open knot. Reaching behind him he attached the open knot onto the vent controller, a piece of metal sticking out at 90 degrees from the wall. Thus prepared, Joe seemed to mumble a last few words to this Magdalena before stepping off the chair.

The noise and ensuing kerfuffle jerked Pat out of his reverie. He saw Joe, sitting on the ground beside an upturned chair, and all around, piled up, and continuing to flop from the vent void, were rolls and rolls of money. Envelopes bulging with cash, wads tied up with brown paper. Joe looked around him uncomprehending.

"What…what the…. this is…I mean, who does this all…..belong to?" Joe looked at the corpses in the room, and whilst unable to put two and two together, he managed to work out a rough equation that resulted in him having a lot of money in front of him. The day had got progressively worse, until it could not get any worse, and then, at the point of obliteration, it suddenly seemed to have got a whole lot better. Joe was unable to process all this logically so did what seemed the best thing to do in the circumstance. He started to laugh. He threw bundles of money about, slapping the floor in his joy.

"Oh, my goodness. Just wait till Lucy hears about this. How long has that money… I mean… was it that bad man's? Was that why he was so very upset?"

Joe stood up and peered up into the void. He could see more money in there. A lot more. The void seemed to go right back into the wall and beyond. He righted the chair and stood on it. Reaching into the cavity he felt around for the money and started to pull great swathes of cash forward into the light. Further in he reached until the snake thought, '*Now might I do it pat*', echoing Hamlet's thoughts of revenging his father. From his hiding place, deep in the void, he lashed out with deadly fangs and bit his tormenter hard on the back of his hand.

"Job done" thought Pat, as he turned away and smelt an exit through an airbrick. Bognor smelt and sounded very interesting. He could discern fresh meat, rats aplenty, even fishy-smelling birds. He was going to enjoy being free in Bognor.

Joe meanwhile realised immediately what had happened.

"Oh blow" he thought. He moved over to his bed and sat on the edge, nursing the throbbing hand. He knew it was terminal – just look at all these dead people

– but he still couldn't decide how he wanted to die. In the end he just sat there and thought of Lucy, running together through the fields of ragwort and poppies in the warm Polish summer. He tried not to think of the Drab's, though he wanted to think of Magdalena, now, at the end. But looking about him, he saw Rosie and then his mind was swamped with the erotic events of earlier. But rather than dash these from his mind he was suddenly overwhelmed by a sense of...calm, warmth.... love. Rosie was very lovely, wasn't she..... Joe sat there, unmoving, unable to act, so far from home. Slow Joe slowed right down. After several hours, his breathing shallowed, and as he imagined him and Rosie stripping off and jumping into the canal to cool off, Joe's big, kind, innocent heart ceased its relentless thump.

Silence.

CHARLIE

Back at the sorting office Charlie had seen a letter to him awaiting delivery. He pulled it out and opened it – it looked official. Maybe it was Student Finance England finally getting its act together and paying him some money to live on! But no, it was from his solicitor, confirming the acceptance of the offer from Gold Properties for his Nan's house. He was gutted. It was worth so much more. He had checked with several

Estate Agents who valued it at three times the amount now showing on the letter. And after fees, capital gains, and sharing out with the family, there'd not be much left. He felt cheated, powerless, and massively let down. It was those bloody squatters that ruined it for him. So why had the local Agent priced it so low? Didn't seem fair.

Despite having finished his round, he was earning extra cash doing special deliveries. He had a few parcels this morning, nothing too big, and he noticed there was one for the Shatalova's at 31b. It was a small box, with a fancy label. Last night he'd gone to Sheiks with a few friends and seen Rosie and that Thin Man, Mr Jones, out on the tiles. She was all over him. Charlie was disgusted, Jones was nearly twice her age. Why wouldn't she look at HIM? They had got very drunk, and Rosie became very lary, which amused his mates when they realised she was the object of his lust. Suffice to say, he was chastened by what he saw and considered NOT bedding Rosie a close encounter. So he approached number 31 with mixed feelings. Considering himself inured against her charms having seen her falling all over the dance floor after 15 tequila slammers, he still had lustful thoughts that remained unfulfilled. He ignored what he presumed was a drunk woman – albeit at first glance a well-dressed drunk, lying unconscious on the pavement in front of the window of 31a. He bounced down the steps as usual, waltzed up to 31b and rapped firmly on the door. When there was no reply, Charlie left the small package in front of the door and returned to the street. But he didn't quite make it. He stopped when he saw the door of 31a open. Unsure what to do, he voiced a simple 'Hello?'. Nothing came back. He stood stock still, but not a sound could be heard. Not even a mouse. So he gingerly pushed at the open door and peered in.

His blood froze at the sight. Everybody he knew in the flat was very much dead. There was blood everywhere. He was momentarily nonplussed to see even the dog had snuffed it. He stepped into the flat and again froze. Another man – one he didn't recognise, but a funny looking bloke with a wonky head, sat bolt upright on the bed, eyes open. Charlie carefully stepped over the bodies – this was a crime scene after all, and he'd seen NSCI on TV – and sat next to the man. He was wearing a dressing cord around his neck with one end attached to what looked like a vent cover.

"You alright?" he asked. Joe didn't reply. Charlie reached out and gently touched Joe on the shoulder. Joe slowly fell back on the bed. Very dead.

"Holy shit" said Charlie, jumping up. He looked around him at the bodies. Rosie and her mother had died in a final embrace. Mr Jones had his face in his briefcase. Charlie examined his feelings. He should be feeling something for these unfortunates, but he noticed with interest he felt nothing. He was shocked, appalled, even disgusted by the range of bodily fluids on show. But these people meant nothing to him, and he knew nothing of how or why they died. But here he was, amongst them all. "I suppose I'd better call the Police" he thought. But just as he reached into his pocket for the phone, his eyes fell upon a huge pile of bank notes underneath a vent on the wall.

The human brain is an amazing thing. Katherine Johnson's brain worked out the maths for getting a rocket to orbit the moon. Einstein's created the theory of relativity, and Paul McCartney wrote 'Yesterday' in a dream. Charlie's brain went through a thousand and one computations in a flash and came up with a clear answer.

He knelt by the pile and scooped as much as he could carry into the post bag over his shoulder, all the while looking over his shoulder. When the bag was full, and he could still close the flap he stood up. There was still plenty of cash on the floor, but he reckoned he had enough. Enough for what he wasn't yet sure, but it was certainly a lot of money weighing down his shoulder. He stood still for a moment, half expecting police, or goons to jump out and arrest or shoot him. But nothing happened. He glanced out of the window, largely obscured by the body of the drunk woman, who was staring in with vacant eyes. She wasn't drunk, she was dead.

Charlie realised it was time to make a hasty exit. He stepped towards the door, making sure he didn't incriminate himself with a bloody footprint. As he passed the table he saw a rather good bottle of wine not quite finished and wondered whether it would be a good idea to take a celebratory swig.